Frenemy Fix-Up

Also by Yahrah St. John

Her Secret Billionaire
Her Best Friend's Brother
Her One Night Consequence

Visit the Author Profile page at Harlequin.com for more titles.

Frenemy Fix-Up

YAHRAH ST. JOHN

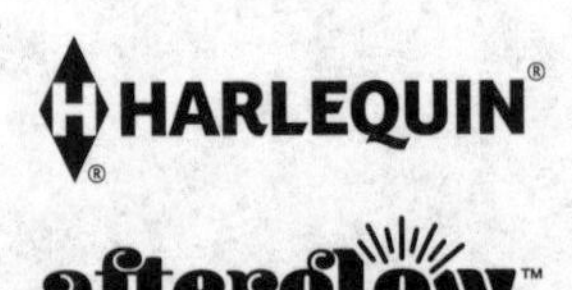

ISBN-13: 978-1-335-04158-6

Frenemy Fix-Up

Harlequin Enterprises ULC
22 Adelaide St. West, 41st Floor
Toronto, Ontario M5H 4E3, Canada
www.Harlequin.com

Printed in U.S.A.

To my publicist, Keisha Mennefee,
for her encouragement and support in
helping me write something new and fresh.

One

SHAY

Rise and flow. Restorative yoga. Abs and booty.

People come to my studio to restore and reset, and hot yoga wasn't supposed to be on offer today. But it's mid-eighties in March and the air-conditioning has gone kaput!

I don't have time for a broken down AC, but that—and a thousand other small things—are what come with being a business owner.

You wanted this, remember?

Yes, I wanted this. I toiled for nine years as a group fitness instructor for some of the largest health-club chains in San Antonio, Texas, but I have always wanted to be my own boss. Set my own hours. Create the environment I *want* to be in. And thanks to an unexpected windfall from my honorary aunt, I renovated and leased *my own* yoga studio.

But I've yet to figure out how to make Balance and Elevate support me with a sustainable income.

When it first opened, I was the only instructor, but once word got out, my regulars left other gyms to come here. Within months, I had to hire two instructors, Dawn and Maribeth, to handle the influx. That allowed the studio to reach its max—good for business, but a strain on overhead. To make the math work, I need to expand.

Luckily, the adjacent suite in this shopping center will be available soon. The bakery owner, Mr. Yang, comes over for free classes, and he shared the news that he'll be leaving when the lease expires. He hasn't told the landlord yet. So if I want the space, now is the time to strike.

My AC unit has other ideas. When it comes to mechanical stuff, I know how to turn it on and off and search for repair companies on my phone. But dealing with clogged toilets and HVAC units is part of owning a business—even when the funds aren't available. Even when I won't turn to my big-time divorce-lawyer brother for help. Even when I *can't* turn to my mama because she's the one who turns to me.

But I don't fall into negative thinking, even when the studio is falling down around me.

Instead, I find a repair company who can make it out within the hour. Of course, they want to charge a trip fee… add it to the bill. My tank top is sticking to my toffee-colored skin and sweat trickles down my yoga pants into unmentionable areas. I pull my long dark brown locs into a quick updo to get them off my neck and crack open the door for a breeze.

But the blast of hot, humid San Antonio air is worse than what's in the building. Soon, the next class will be ending, and Dawn won't have anywhere to cool down. It's a sweltering eighty-five degrees inside, and it's not even noon. By late afternoon, it'll likely be close to a hundred. Frozen drinks are what we need on a day like today. I grab my purse and head to the nearby smoothie place located several doors down.

I don't bother changing my attire because I'll be sweating until the repairman arrives. Who am I going to see?

I sigh with relief when I open the door of the smoothie shop and a cool blast of air hits my skin. It's nearly lunchtime, and there are several people in line. A few extra minutes of AC is a win.

As I'm deciding what to get, someone bumps into me. I spin around, folding my arms across my chest, waiting for an apology. None is forthcoming.

The perpetrator is one of those corporate types, earbuds in, his forehead creased in a frown, deep in thought if the firm line of his mouth is any indication. Yet, confidence radiates from his tall frame. The jacket sleeves of his blue suit are pushed back and his black and silver tie is loose. The color of his skin makes me think about rich honey; his full lips surrounded by a sexy five-o'clock shadow make me think about the rasp against my inner thighs if his face were buried deep between them.

Jesus, am I really thinking this way about a stranger?

Yeah, because since my divorce, there haven't been many opportunities to get busy with anyone except my vibrator. Lord knows, I've worn the poor thing out.

While I'm not deliberately celibate, avoiding the opposite sex equals avoiding bad luck in the love department. I don't usually dwell on the downside, but the truth is love isn't all it's cracked up to be. Exhibit A: my father ran out on the family when I was young. Exhibit B: my brother Riley hightailed it off to college and law school, leaving me to care for Mama. Exhibit C: my short-lived marriage, an epic failure.

Much safer to ogle Mr. Corporate and wonder what he's packing beneath those clothes.

And since he can't be bothered to say *excuse me*, I spin around on my heel and face forward. "Jerk," I say out loud.

"What did you just call me?"

I spin around again. "You heard what I..."

The remaining words evaporate as his heavy-lidded gaze makes contact with mine. An unfamiliar sensation slithers from my abdomen into places that have been dormant for too long. My cheeks warm.

I *know* him.

Colin Anderson.

Aka my first crush. Aka the boy who completely ignored me in high school. *What the hell is he doing here?* Didn't he move away?

He steps backward to regard me. His eyes travel from my sneakers up my snug-fitting Lululemon cayenne-colored yoga pants to my keyhole sports bra before finally landing on my brown eyes. My face flushes. "Do you always come out of the house half-naked?"

Anger flares inside me. *He* bumps into *me*, and now he wants to criticize what I'm wearing? "Are you always this rude?" When he begins to speak, I continue. "It was a rhetorical question. Earlier, I called you a *jerk*, and I stand behind the comment."

"Ouch!" He touches his chest. "If your goal was to wound me, you missed your mark."

"That's too bad," I respond. "Wonder what it would take to knock that giant-sized chip off your shoulder, Colin."

His brows furrow. "How do you know my name?"

I roll my eyes and turn away just as the worker at the counter is ready to take my order. "I'll have the Detox smoothie and an Acai Berry Boost."

"Coming right up."

Within seconds, I'm all paid up and moving to the side to wait for my order. I ignore Colin like he used to ignore me. He was rude back then and clearly hasn't grown out of it. His eyes burn the back of my skull until his phone rings and he's forced to answer it—just before coming to the counter.

Rude.

I keep my head low and play Wordle on my phone. I ignore the approaching footsteps until he's standing directly in front of me.

"How do you know me?" Colin demands—because he sure as hell doesn't ask.

I hazard a quick glance at him before returning to my phone. "I don't owe you an explanation."

He won't let it go.

"Yes, you do. You just called me a *jerk* and insinuated I have a giant ego." Colin frowns. "You don't even know me."

I shrug. I know enough.

"So that's it?" He folds his muscled arms across his broad chest. "You're really not going to tell me who you are?"

Part of me wants him to stew, to wonder exactly who I am. But what purpose will that serve?

His dark enigmatic eyes are trained on me.

"I'm Shay. Shay Davis."

"Wait a second." He points at me. "Didn't we go to high school together?"

"We did indeed."

"And you thought I was arrogant back then?" he asks, rubbing his chin.

"Well, this interaction certainly hasn't changed that opinion."

He cocks his head to one side, watching me. "Did something happen between us in high school?"

"Of course you wouldn't remember me. You were all about Claire Watson. She wasn't a nice person, and you know what they say, *birds of a feather...*"

Colin steps into my personal space, and I catch a faint whiff of his cologne. It's earthy, and heady.

"You didn't know Claire like I did. She can be amazing."

I huff, and his eyes narrow.

"Perhaps you should get to know someone before making snap judgments, Shay. If I recall, not everyone thought highly of your little clique either."

"Don't talk about my girls," I warn. I'm fiercely protective of the women I consider my sisters: Wynter, Egypt, Asia, Lyric and Teagan. We call ourselves the Six Gems. They've gotten me through the worst of times. From my parents' divorce when were teenagers to my ill-fated early marriage and subsequent divorce from Kevin.

"You started us down this path, Shay," Colin responds.

"Number seven," the cashier calls.

That's my number. I push past Colin, grab both smoothies and head outside. I hear my name but don't turn around and instead keep going until I get to the studio, where I open the door and walk inside. Several women are already in the lounge area waiting for the next class to begin.

Colin fills the doorway and then navigates through the throng of women until he reaches me. "What is this place?"

It should be clear, but I answer, "It's my yoga studio. You know, where people come to take classes for fitness. Or to relieve stress. And from the looks of it, you could use a stress-relieving class."

He glares at me. "What's that supposed to mean?"

Without even thinking, I walk toward him and touch his shoulders. Strong and wide. Heat emanates from him to me. I ignore it.

"Your shoulders are hunched. And your posture is terrible." I walk around to face him. "You were tense during that conversation earlier. The strain was all over your face, from your forehead to your mouth." And oh, what a mouth it is, surrounded by that almost-beard. "You should consider taking a class. It might improve your health."

His eyes flare. "Don't tell me what to do. Besides, I'm too busy at work to spare time for all this." He motions with his hands to the room, marking my life's work as insignificant.

"That's too bad because it might help relieve the stress you're under."

"You think I'm stressed?"

"Aren't you?" I shrug. "If you keep allowing work to consume you, you won't make it to fifty. I've worked in the fitness industry for a decade, and corporate types, just like you, have had heart attacks at a young age. Heart disease is the leading killer of men in America. Just trying to help. Though, quite frankly, you're not my business."

I'm one to talk about not letting work consume you. I've been working night and day to make B&E successful. It hasn't been easy. But I have the benefit of my own classes to keep me balanced.

"Don't try to scare me with your new-age mumbo jumbo. Yoga isn't even real exercise," Colin says.

"Right. Don't listen to me," I reply. "I'm only certified in fitness and nutrition," I add hotly. "But I don't have time to argue with you. Class is starting, for people who value my expertise."

I start to move away, but Colin touches my arm. The action, although small, is electrifying. My heart rate speeds up. His dark eyes are hooded, and I can't tell if he felt the spark too.

"I have to go," I say again, snatching my arm away.

"You're very opinionated, Shay Davis," Colin replies, "and judgmental. If I had the time..." His voice trails off, but his dark eyes shamelessly stare at me.

My stomach tightens. In anticipation? I don't know, but I don't back down. "You would do what?"

His full lips twist upward slightly. "I would teach you a lesson." His gaze goes to my mouth this time, and there's no mistaking what he means. He would kiss me...and more. I'm certain of it. The atmosphere throbs, and I remind myself he's a jerk. And I'm not interested in relationships.

"As if," I snort, turn on my heel and don't look back.

Colin Anderson is not the boy I used to know. He's a stunningly beautiful man who, although arrogant, could make me want to forget swearing off men.

It's good this was just a passing encounter. I have classes to teach and a repairman to pay, and B&E takes priority over any fleeting attraction.

After class and AC repairs and way too much time spent thinking about what it would feel like to have the bruising weight of Colin's mouth on mine, I drive over to my mama's. Because of her battle with mental health, I often check in on her.

When I pull into her driveway, my brother Riley's Lamborghini Urus is already there. It's flashy and bold and nothing like my Hyundai Sonata, which is all I can afford. Riley offered to upgrade me since he's a hotshot attorney. He feels guilty because I've been Mama's sole caregiver for the last decade, while he was away making partner. Now that he's back in San Antonio, he wants to help me too. But I'm used to taking care of myself and have politely declined.

Turning off the ignition, I use my key and enter Mama's. She and Riley are in the kitchen holding glasses of wine. I am happy to see them huddled together. They both have dark brown hair, but that's where the similarities end. Riley's is closely cropped and Mama's is shoulder-length. Their eyes are different too. Hers are dark brown like mine, while his take after our father with his ebony irises. He's dressed in trousers and a crisp white shirt, like he just came from work, while she is in jeans and a tank top.

"Hey, Mama." I walk over and press my lips to her cheek.

"Riley." I give him a kiss on his cheek too. "What are you doing here? I thought you would be with Wynter finalizing Operation Wedding."

Riley is marrying my best friend in two months. There's still a lot to be done according to the daily texts from Wynter.

"Ha," he lets out a laugh. "That's exactly why I'm here." He towers over me at six foot three. "Mrs. Barrington's endless chatter about place settings and menus for the rehearsal dinner drove me away. I honestly could care less. All I want to do is marry the woman I love."

"Wynter wants that too."

"Yeah, but the fuss the Barringtons are making over this wedding..."

"It's their way of making it up to Wynter," I offer. "They messed up when they turned against her at the reading of Helaine's will." The Barringtons and Wynter had a falling-out after the reading of her aunt's will: Wynter was the main beneficiary, and her aunt left each of the Six Gems an inheritance.

I loved Wynter's aunt. Helaine was a shoulder to lean on when I needed to vent about Mama, about missing Riley, about having so much responsibility at a young age. She gave me advice and guidance I didn't get anywhere else. And the gift of her inheritance was such a blessing. Prospects of starting my own business were bleak until that windfall. There weren't enough classes or training that would have brought in the funds to cover B&E's renovation and rent.

"I wish they would figure out another way to show their penance other than driving me and my fiancée batshit crazy."

I laugh and head to the counter. Opening the drawer, I pull out a stopper, place it over the wine and put the bottle back into the double-sided Samsung refrigerator.

"Sweetheart, we're still drinking that," Mama replies.

"You know alcohol can have a negative effect with your antidepressants." I give Riley a pointed stare because he brought over the bottle. He doesn't know the effects of mixing liquor with meds because he wasn't around when the meds were prescribed. I love him, but part of me hasn't forgiven him for his disappearing act, leaving all of Mama's care to me. He's making amends now, but it's still frustrating.

"I'm sorry, Shay," Riley responds. "Mom and I were celebrating my latest case. I won custody for a mother who fought her abusive ex-husband for their daughter".

"That's great, Riley. Way to go."

"I should be able to celebrate," Mama replies, stuck on the fact I put the wine away. "You don't have to treat me like a child, Shay."

But you're acting like one.

I glare at her. Looking out for Mama is ingrained in me and has been since I was a teenager. But it's exhausting. And I can't believe her attitude. After everything I've done. After everything I've given up. My marriage may not have been the greatest, but taking care of her was one of the reasons it failed.

When will it be my time?

"Don't give me that look, Shay," Mama adds. "The last few years, I've stayed on my antidepressants and followed the program."

"Yes, you have." It's the what-ifs I worry about. What if

she has an episode, sending her careening back into depression? After all these years, she is self-sufficient, and that's a load off my shoulders. I have more freedom now than I had growing up.

"Then, give me some breathing room," she responds.

My eyes lock with hers for several moments, then I rush out the French doors leading to the terrace, getting emotional. I need some air. For years, I've watched Mama—loving her, not wanting to lose her…and afraid of becoming her. She let my father's rejection destroy her. With our family history, I know I'm susceptible to depression. I have to be strong. Keep my mind, body and soul in top shape, reduce stress.

Several minutes later, the doors open, and Riley joins me. I stare at the night sky.

"She is doing better, Shay."

"That's easy for you to say, Riley," I snap. "You weren't here."

He nods. "I deserve that. I deserve all your anger. I left you alone to deal with Mama's depression and erratic behavior."

My eyes narrow. "Yes, you did."

"I was selfish," Riley says. "I didn't know how to go to college, enjoy life and still be the man of the house."

Tears well in my eyes. "I know, Riley. When Mama fell to pieces after Daddy left, you were a child too."

"But I was the oldest. I failed you, Shay, and all these years you've let me off the hook. You should be giving me the business."

"What would be the point? It won't change things. We can't go back. We can only face forward. Like how I dive into my work with Balance and Elevate. It's my way of coping."

"I get it, but it might make me feel better if you let me have it," Riley says with a chuckle.

"You would be getting off easy," I respond with a laugh. "I'd rather you suffer a little bit."

"Ouch." Riley reaches for me, pulling me into a warm hug. He's so tall, his chin rests on top of my head. "She just wants a bit more freedom."

"And I want her to have it, but I—I can't pick her up off the ground again, Riley. Been there. Done that. I'm tired. Like you, I want a life too."

He lifts his head and looks down at me, but he doesn't let go. "I wholeheartedly agree. You've done so much, given up so much. I want you to have a full life and meet the man of your dreams who adores you as much as I do Wynter."

A full life? What does that even mean? I have one. I have my family. My business. The Gems. That's enough, right? Am I incomplete without a man? No. But that doesn't stop my mind from wandering to Colin. I sigh with frustration. Why is he in my head? I don't want him there. He's not *the man of my dreams.*

He's just the first man in long time to make me feel… an attraction.

"Thanks, Riley," I say, telling him what he wants to hear. "And I will do my best to ease up on Mama, but I don't like her mixing wine and medications."

"Duly noted. I'll do better next time, but let her enjoy tonight, okay?"

"Fine." Shrugging, we go back inside, and I put on the

conciliatory expression I'm expected to wear, but deep down, I worry. Mama's depressive episodes are long and taxing. I know how bad it can get when she's in a downward spiral. Maybe it won't happen again. Maybe I can enjoy this special time in our lives because my brother is marrying my best friend.

And no matter what, I'll work on expanding Balance and Elevate, finally adding the Pilates studio I've always wanted. As for Colin, any images that pop into my head, I'll banish them.

My legacy will be bringing in more customers, to make B&E the success I know it can be.

I won't stop until I make it happen.

Two

COLIN

Shay Davis is smoking hot.

There's no other way to describe her.

Sitting in my office in downtown San Antonio, I think about our exchange yesterday. On the surface, it was fiery, but underneath there was something else…

Attraction.

I haven't felt it in a long time because I've been working sixty-to-eighty-hour weeks. The company where I'm controller, the Myers Group, is going public. I've put in a lot of time to make sure the financials are up to par. A few more weeks and my life can go back to some semblance of normalcy. Although, if I'm honest, my normal doesn't differ much from the hours I've put in recently.

The IPO's success and my role in it will propel me to the executive level and being director of accounting. A burning desire to succeed, to be the best at everything, was ingrained in me by my father, Wade Anderson, a successful car salesman and dealership owner.

He was a self-made man who came from nothing, never accepted second-best. He pushed me to excel in school so I could have a better life than he did. If I got a B, he demanded to know why I didn't get an A. When I joined the basketball team to have fun and enjoy the camaraderie of the team, my father ordered, "You will make varsity."

Or I would die trying.

He passed away three years ago, and yet his voice still lives inside me, pushing me.

Focusing all my attention on my career has left little time for pleasure. Is that why I can't stop daydreaming about Shay Davis, the sexy yoga-studio owner with the hot body? When I saw her at the smoothie shop, my eyes roamed every inch of her curves. She had on a skimpy tank top revealing round breasts. Her yoga pants left *nothing* to the imagination and looked as if they'd been spray-painted on. I got hard the instant she turned away and I caught a glimpse of her ass.

Christ! On any given Sunday, I would never go for a hippie girl like Shay. My type is refined, classic, with a similar corporate career, someone I can take home to my mom. My father always told me it matters who you date and who you marry.

My parents were married thirty years, until the day he died. I want a marriage like theirs. It was built on love, trust and adoration. My dad used to look at Mom as if she were the most beautiful woman in the world.

I felt that way once about Claire Watson.

Ah, Claire.

The one who got away.

Claire had been the most popular girl at the public high school we attended. Unlike Shay—who lived in a middle-class neighborhood and, rumor had it, lived without the father who'd walked out on her mother—Claire fit my profile. She came from an affluent family with a two-parent household, like me. She broke my heart in college, yet I've measured every woman against her ever since, now including Shay.

The sexy yoga teacher. Limber and flexible and probably knows all kind of positions—

My cell phone rings loudly on the desk. Damn. It's my sister, Thea. I swipe right. Her beautiful brown face lights up the screen. "Hey, sis, what's up?"

"Your phone isn't broken?" she asks. Her dark brown braids are in an elaborate updo on top of her head.

"Don't be sarcastic." Thea is three years younger, and I've always felt protective of her. Whenever boys came to the house to see her, they'd have to talk to me first. Her husband, Bradley, is the only man I've ever approved of because he worked for my father and was his right hand at the dealership. With Dad gone, it was up to me to ensure Bradley was good enough for my baby sister.

"I've called you for weeks and you've been MIA, Colin."

"I'm sorry, Thea. I've been busy at work. This IPO has everyone on edge, including me."

"When does the company go public?"

"In a few weeks. Then I'll get my life back."

"And you'll come see your family?" my sister says. "You've only visited your niece once, and she's already three months old." Thea holds up Kira in her arms. Kira is wearing a pink onesie that says *Daddy's Girl*. My heart does a somersault at seeing her chubby cheeks.

"She's beautiful, Thea."

"Thank you."

I feel guilty about my absence. Other than my initial hospital visit and once at their house, I haven't been by. I'm excited to be an uncle, but work has taken precedence. "I'll do better, I promise."

"You'd better. Otherwise, you'll look up and Kira will be walking and talking, and you'll have missed it."

"Agreed. I'll stop by this weekend. How does that sound?"

"Don't make promises you're not going to keep," Thea replies sharply.

"Have I really been that unreliable?"

"Yeah."

"I mean it this time."

"You said that before," Thea chides. "You can't let work consume you, Colin, to the exclusion of everything else. You're thirty and already a workaholic. It will only get worse if you don't make time for balance."

Shay preached the same thing to me yesterday. Is this the universe trying to tell me something? I've been burning the midnight oil for the last year, but once the IPO is over, my schedule will relax. Post IPO won't nearly be at the same breakneck speed.

I hope.

"I understand, and I agree with you. I promise I will stop by on Saturday."

"Why not tomorrow?"

"I have to work. We're getting ready for the road show."

Thea laughs. "Road show? You're an accountant."

"That's the term we use to describe face-to-face meetings with potential investors in various cities. We introduce the company, our history and key management personnel to build enthusiasm for the public offering."

"How do they do that?"

"Usually, there's a video presentation with our unique value proposition, earnings and financial performance, prior sales growth and future projections, and of course the stock-price target."

"Sounds exhausting," Thea says, her voice softening. "I'm seriously worried about you, especially after Daddy."

"That's not fair, Thea."

"Why the hell not? He died from a heart attack, Colin. An attack that could have been avoided if he'd taken better care of himself. He was always at the dealership."

"Listen, I've heard everything you've said. You don't have to beat a dead horse."

"Fine. As long as you promise I'll see you this weekend."

I hold up three fingers with my palm face out. "Scout's honor."

"You hated being a Boy Scout because you hated the outdoors and getting dirty."

I chuckle because Thea is absolutely right. I wasn't an outdoors kid, but sit me in front of a computer and I was a whiz. "You get my drift."

Thea smiles on the screen. "Yes, I do, and I'll see you then. Love you." She lifts Kira's palm so she can wave at me too.

"Love you both." I end the call and lean back in my chair. Thea has a point. I will do better.

As soon as the IPO is over.

Several days later, I arrive to the office early to finalize the Myers Group's first road show. We are headed to the Waldorf Astoria in New York City next week, and I need to be sure everything is in order. We've already filed with the SEC, but that's step one.

We don't have a director of accounting, so as controller, I've spearheaded the IPO. There's a lot of pressure to ensure the road show goes off without a hitch. After NYC will be Boston, Chicago, Los Angeles, San Francisco, London, Hong Kong and Singapore. The Myers Group wants to be seen as an international company with a global reach.

Even though it's not my job, I ask the communications team to send me the video and slideshow. I head to PR and make sure the attendee gift bags have the right logo. We've invited over two hundred investors. This is a big deal, and I'll soon see the fruits of my labor.

Matt Harris, my coworker and assistant controller, stops in my doorway. He is my competition. Yet, we've always managed to be friendly and have a good working relationship. Matt is a young, affable blond with a penchant for wearing his short hair in a crew cut and dressing in a suit with a colorful pocket square. "Do you ever go home?" he inquires.

"Can't," I respond. "Too much to do."

"You're going to burn yourself out, Colin," Matt replies, echoing what everyone seems to be saying to me these days. "Once the IPO is over, there'll be more work. Pace yourself. When was the last time you had fun or even went out on a date?"

Leaning back in my chair, I try to think back. Somehow this IPO has taken over my life.

I shrug. "Can't remember."

"Exactly," Matt says. "Which means it's been too long. When the IPO is over, make time for yourself."

I nod. "Sure thing." It's the answer Matt's looking for, and seconds later he's gone.

It's not like I haven't thought about dating. Last night, lying in bed, sex was all I could think about. One woman came to mind, and she wasn't Claire. I dreamed of Shay, dark locs flung back and her perky breasts moving, as she rode me fast and hard. When I woke up this morning, I couldn't rid my mind of the image.

My body wants her. My mind knows she isn't my type. Yes, she's sexy. I can't deny that, especially when she wears skimpy workout attire, but when I'm ready to date, I want a woman like Claire. I hear my father's voice telling me, "It matters who you marry." I've always wanted to please him.

Even now. Even though he's gone.

Poised, beautiful, educated Claire.

A woman who can stand beside me and mingle with the executives. A woman who can have my babies, be head of the PTA and be a freak in the bedroom. Shay Davis, however, is a rebel. She dances to the beat of her own drum. My instincts tell me she won't do the expected.

The thought unsettles me.

I have always done the expected. Because my father demanded it. Because it's who I am. Failure is not an option.

As the eldest, I excelled in school, had perfect attendance, joined the National Honor Society and made the honor roll every semester. When it was time for college, I went to a school with the best accounting program in Texas.

Because I had to be the best.

In everything. Including who I date.

Shaking off thoughts of the sexy yoga trainer, I return my focus to work. Hours pass before I finally turn off my laptop and decide to head home.

When I arrive at the elevators, the vice president, Craig Abbott, is waiting too.

"Good evening, Craig."

"Burning the midnight oil?" Craig asks. He's an easygoing man of average height, with floppy brown hair. He's in his usual suit and tie, loosened at the collar.

"Yes, sir. I'm ready for the IPO."

"You've worked hard enough, Colin," Craig says. "If I were a betting man, I would say big changes are ahead for you when we go public."

"Thank you, sir." I'm brimming with excitement, but I keep my expression neutral. Craig is all business, and he didn't have to hint at a promotion. But he did. My hard work isn't going unrecognized.

The elevator arrives, and we step in.

On the way down, Craig surprises me by asking, "Do you play golf? Dan, Josh and I," he says, naming the CEO and CFO at the Myers Group, "are catching some sun and tossing a few balls. Would be great to have a fourth. Would you be interested?"

I'm not turning down an invitation to play with the big boys. "Only a handful of times."

"I have a golf instructor who will single-handedly change your stroke," Craig replies. "Come on Saturday. We start around eight a.m."

Saturday?

Damn. I promised Thea I would stop by, but an opportunity like this may not come again. I have to seize the moment. "I'm there. Just let me know the address."

"Excellent. I'll have my assistant send you the details."

Once at the garage level, Craig pats my shoulder and exits. I walk to my Audi in a daze. Hard work and dedication does pay off. Just like my father said.

After I play golf, I can see Thea and Kira. My sister will understand. She'll show me a little grace because it's not every day you get a chance to shatter the glass ceiling.

Three

SHAY

"What do you think, Shay?" Wynter asks late Saturday morning at the bridal store.

I stare at my reflection in the A-line one-shoulder floor-length chiffon bridesmaid dress.

"It's lovely," I respond. Months ago, they didn't have my size and I ordered sight unseen, but I'm pleased with the result.

Wynter called and suggested we spend quality time together. We both live in San Antonio, but the last few months I've been busy building Balance and Elevate while Wynter has been planning her wedding. She doesn't need a piece of paper to prove what I already know: she's my sister.

"I love how it shows off your svelte figure." Wynter eyes me in the dress.

"I wish I had more curves like you."

Wynter is what men call a *brick house*. At five feet two,

she has full breasts and curvaceous hips, while I, at five foot four, could use a few extra curves. My breasts are small and barely manage to fill a B cup. While I may not have Wynter's pear-shaped bum with an itty-bitty waist, I have always loved my ass. It's round and looks damn good in a pair of yoga pants.

"Shay, I would kill for your figure," Wynter says, "and your taut abs. Why can't we women love the bodies we're in?"

"I don't know, girlfriend. It's a curse. Never satisfied. But this dress is killer." It shows off my athletic legs through a slit in the chiffon. "I love the peekaboo thigh."

"It might help you snag a fella," Wynter says with a wink. "Riley invited several men from his practice to the wedding."

"Oh lord, not you too." Ever since Riley got engaged, he's been trying to fix me up.

"Can I help it that I'm in love and want the same thing for my sister?" Wynter says, shrugging her shoulders.

Stepping off the dais, I lean in for a hug. "Of course not. I know it comes from a good place."

"It does. First me, now Egypt and Asia are both engaged. It must be difficult for you."

Her suggestion strikes a nerve. Six months ago, our friend Egypt got engaged to Garrett Forrester, and Asia recently announced she's pregnant by her one-night stand and she's engaged now too. Each of my Gems are getting hitched one by one. I've been married before. It's easy to fall in love. It's harder to stay in love.

"Of course," I finally say. "The divorce was tough. It made me doubt whether I want to get married again or have a family someday. Then—surprise, surprise!—Asia gets a two-for-one."

It hurts that Asia wasn't trying to get pregnant and did so easily. When Kevin and I were trying for a baby, I struggled. I had two miscarriages—both brutal, physically and emotionally. Somehow I feel guilty for not carrying my babies to term, as if I failed, as if I weren't strong enough. I never shared the depth of my losses with the Gems. It still feels…private.

I square my shoulders. I'm fit and healthy now. That's all that matters.

Wynter's hand reaches for mine. "I figured as much, but you can talk to me, to any of us."

"I know. But it's hard to believe Mr. Wonderful will come along." Wynter is hopeful because she's desperately in love with Riley, but I don't have the time or energy to give to a relationship. My focus is on the studio becoming a success while keeping a watchful eye on my mama.

"Don't give up, Shay. Why not consider the men at Riley's practice?" Wynter responds. "Ya know, keep your options open?"

When I think about options, my mind wanders to Colin at the smoothie shop and how good he looked. *Why am I still thinking about him?* He is yesterday's news. A blip from my past, nothing more. Besides, he thinks yoga and fitness—my life's work—is overrated.

"Shay, are you holding out on me?" Wynter stares at me.

"What are you talking about?" I frown and try to move away, but her eyes are trained on mine.

"Have you met someone?"

"Not really. I mean, I had a run-in the other day with someone we know. Colin Anderson."

"*The Colin* you had a crush on in high school for, like, *ever*? You mean *that* Colin?"

"I don't want to talk about Colin."

Or the way he made me feel—then or now. How I'd been burningly aware of his presence only a few feet away as we stood in line—the scent of his aftershave and the sheer masculinity of him. Or the drumming beat of my pulse and tightening of my lungs even as I insulted him. It's crazy I'm feeling this way about a guy I haven't seen in over a decade. And a jerk at that!

"Okay," Wynter says with a smile.

A sigh of relief escapes my lips because she let it go. Once I've slipped off the dress, I put on my usual tank top and yoga pants for our lunch.

One day, I want my own line of activewear. That wasn't always my dream. Before the miscarriages, before the divorce, I dreamed of having a home and a family of my own. But grief has a way of making things fall apart, like marriages. Now my sights are on a future that includes fitness fashion.

At the nearby outdoor café down the street, I share the concept with Wynter.

"Shay, that sounds great. Who better than you, a fitness instructor, to design activewear? Have you talked to any companies about distribution or manufacturing? Who would design the clothing?"

I shake my head vigorously. "No, not yet. And I have

some ideas on design. My focus is on expanding the yoga studio at the moment."

"By adding Pilates?"

Last time the Gems got together, I mentioned my desire to include Pilates and make Balance and Elevate a one-stop shop for fitness geeks such as myself. "The store next door is closing in a few months, and I want to take the space."

"I'm so proud of you, Shay. My aunt is smiling down at you because you're making your dream come true."

Tears well in my eyes. "Aunt Helaine's gift was a miracle, Wynter. I don't think you know how appreciative I am."

"My auntie loved you as much I do. She thought of us all as her daughters because she never had children of her own."

"You miss her, don't you?"

"All the time. I never realized what a big role she played in my life until she wasn't there." Wynter sniffs, wiping away a tear. "I would give anything to have her by my side when I marry the love of my life."

"She sees you. Just like she sees the dreams we Gems are making reality because of the gifts she left us. Your travel magazine and YouTube channel are a success, Egypt has her restaurant, Asia is opening her store, I have the yoga studio, Teagan's brokerage business is booming, and Lyric's dance spot will be open shortly."

"Who would have thought two years would make such a difference?"

I laugh out loud. "I sure didn't. I thought I'd be toiling at someone else's gym forever. Being my own boss has pushed me out of my comfort zone, but it's also taught me how to be self-reliant. That's important."

"Because of your mom?"

I nod. Wynter knows me so well. "I'm happy she's doing well right now, but I can't help worrying that something will set her off. I'm always waiting for the other shoe to drop. But it's gotten easier now that Riley is here. Not all the responsibility falls on my shoulders. I can take a breath and focus on me for a change."

Wynter nods. "Riley is committed to being there for you and your mom."

"Good. Because things are finally moving for me, and nothing will stop me from achieving my goals."

Later that evening at my apartment, after making myself a quinoa salad, I curl up with my laptop and crunch the numbers on the expansion. Memberships are up, thanks to great reviews and references from my current clientele. It's gratifying to see folks appreciating all the hard work I put in designing the studio and building it from the ground up.

Unfortunately, the numbers don't look good. More capital is required for the Pilates expansion. Last time, the renovation took a lot more money than I anticipated. How do I raise more money? I could ask Riley, but B&E is my baby.

Tossing my laptop onto the couch, I take some deep, calming breaths. *Center yourself, Shay. No negative thoughts.* In the back of my mind, I worry that if I take on too much stress, I might break. Like Mama did when my father left her for another woman.

She couldn't cope and checked out of our family. When my father came back to pack his belongings, I wanted to yell at him, to ask why he didn't stay. I felt abandoned, but damned if I would show it. Mama, however, fell to her knees, pleading and begging. “Don’t leave me,” she said. “Stay with me.” He didn’t listen and left anyway. Riley picked Mama off the floor and helped her to her room where she stayed for months. I was scared, but I thought that as long as the three of us were together we’d be okay.

But then Riley left for college, deserting us just like my father had. And now that I’m older, I get it. He was starting an exciting new chapter in his life, one full of hope and promise. *But what about me?* I was only fourteen and Mom’s episodes of depression were up and down. Predicting what might set her off was impossible. Finding the Gems in high school was a godsend. My friends gave me the outlet I needed to still be me.

Blinking, I return to the present. Allowing fear of the unknown to prevent me from achieving my goals is a defeatist attitude, one that I reject on instinct. But the increase in rent, the renovation expansion and the upkeep on equipment will all be added challenges. What I really need is someone good with numbers who can help me figure out a way to expand without going broke.

Colin.

He was always good with numbers.

But he isn’t an option. He doesn’t believe in what I do. Health and fitness are everything to me. I’m breaking the cycle and will have a healthier life than Mama did. And if Colin mocks my career and my passion, then I don’t need him.

Four

COLIN

When I arrive at Thea's house on Saturday evening, it's well after eight o'clock, and Kira is most likely sleeping. I would have come earlier, but spending time with the vice president, CEO and CFO paid off. We laughed and cracked jokes and I relaxed with them—enough that they took me into their confidence and admitted they think very highly of me.

"You can go far," Dan Myers said, "but if you ask me, if you want to be taken seriously, you need to get a wife. Shows us you're stable and in a committed relationship."

The advice felt old-school, but the Myers Group is a traditional place. And mulling over his words, I wonder if he's right. Yet the only woman I can conjure up is Shay, and she won't do. Not only does she not seem to like me, she's also too new-age to fit in with this group of corporate types. I need a woman who can stand by my side in a room with the Dan Myerses and Craig Abbots of the world, not help them stretch out in a yoga pose.

Yet, I can't stop thinking about Shay. In high school she was always quiet around me. She didn't have the spunk and fire she has now. My body *wants* her. This is merely a physical response to going so long without sex, without kissing and being skin-to-skin. These feelings are unwanted, especially with the IPO in the works. They go against all the plans I've set for my career.

For my future.

That I can't stop thinking about her makes me feel…out of control. Which is unlike me. I've always followed the plan, the guidelines my father taught me. And somehow, Shay makes me want to chuck it all. Frustration fills my chest.

I don't have time for this kind of distraction.

I'll go to her studio tomorrow and prove this attraction is all in my head. Or we'll fuck and I'll get it out of my system.

There's no in-between.

Now, though, I put thoughts of Shay aside. Again.

Staring up at Thea's adorable Craftsman three-bedroom, I suspect she's going to read me the riot act. I climb out of my Audi Q5 Sportsback and ring the doorbell. Thea takes several minutes to answer, but when she does, there is no mistaking the glower on her honey-nut brown face.

"I thought you were coming hours ago, Colin. I've already put Kira to bed." Suddenly, I hear a low wail from inside, and her eyes narrow. "And now the doorbell has woken her up. Thanks a lot."

"I'm sorry."

"Yeah, you're sorry." She turns on her heel without bothering to invite me in. Her braids swing as she runs up the stairs. Stepping inside, I don't bother following her. Thea has a mean streak a mile wide, and I'd rather she cools down than be on the receiving end. Instead, I head down the corridor to the family room at the back of the house. My brother-in-law is standing by the kitchen island.

"Hey, Colin." Bradley gives me a one-armed hug. "Glad you could finally join us."

"Not you too," I say, rolling my eyes.

He shrugs. "You told Thea you were coming earlier, did you not?"

"Yeah, I did. Listen…" I start to speak, but I stop as I realize there's another person in the room, sitting at the kitchen island. A person I haven't seen in years. No, make that a decade.

It's none other than Claire Watson.

"Claire?"

She nods and inclines her head toward me. "Colin."

I can't believe it's her. In the flesh. She's been on my mind lately, and she materializes out of the clear blue? I stare dumbfounded at my ideal woman. At five foot nine, with a slender figure, she complements my six-foot height. She has beautiful brown eyes and smooth skin the color of ginger, and her teeth are perfectly straight. Her mane of honey-brown hair hangs luxuriously down her back and is nothing like Shay's dark brown locs.

Why am I even thinking about Shay? Claire is everything I'd ever wanted. Even her outfit screams *classy*. She's wearing an off-the-shoulder taupe sweater and black slacks. Meeting her tonight is fortuitous. Exactly the push I need.

According to Dan, if I'm in a committed relationship, the higher-ups will look at me differently. Consider me for the executive level. I can break that glass ceiling.

"Colin?" Claire snaps me out of my musings.

I blink several times. "Sorry. I'm just surprised to see you here."

"I ran into Thea the other day at the grocery store, and she mentioned you were coming over for dinner and, well..." She doesn't need to finish because of course I fucked it up by *not* coming to dinner.

"I had a business meeting that ran over."

Her eyebrow rises. "On a Saturday? Do you make it a habit of working on weekends?"

Smiling awkwardly, I respond, "Not usually, but my company is going public, and this was an opportunity to bump shoulders with the higher-ups."

"That's too bad. I was looking forward to seeing you, but now I have to go." She stands and reaches for her purse.

"So early?" My watch displays eight fifteen.

"Yeah, me and my girls are going out later, and I need to get ready. It was good seeing you again." Before I know it, she's thanking Bradley and heading down the corridor while I remain frozen in place.

Bradley inclines his head toward her retreating figure, and I spring into action. I catch her in the hall before she reaches the front door. "Claire, wait!"

She turns, and her mane of honey-colored hair swishes over her shoulder. "Yes?"

"I'm sorry I was late, but perhaps we could meet up another time? I'd love to catch up, see what you've been up to all these years."

She frowns. "It sounds like you have a lot on your plate, Colin."

"I do, but I can make room."

"Can you? You've always been driven to succeed. I saw it when were in high school, and college too. When is it ever enough?"

Her words gut me because I assumed her coming here meant she was interested in rekindling a relationship. Or am I missing something?

"You make success sound like a bad thing."

"It isn't, but you have to know how to balance it," Claire responds.

Why does everyone in my life keep mentioning *balance*? Why aren't they commenting on my successes?

During our conversation, Thea descends the stairs. "Claire, are you leaving?"

"Dinner was lovely. Thank you for inviting me, but I have another engagement."

Thea sighs. "Oh, to be single and footloose. I remember those days."

Claire laughs, and the sound is a melody to my ears. "You have everything I want," Claire replies, fanning her arm around. "A beautiful home, a loving husband and a brand-new baby."

That's exactly what I want too. Or at least someday. If Claire is here, somehow back in my life *and* ready to settle down, now is the time for us to start over. In college, she'd wanted to see other people, said we were too young to be so serious, but time has passed. Sure, things are heating up at the office, but I *can* balance work and life—no matter what everyone seems to think. Especially if I have Claire to come home to. Imagine how great she would look on my arm at company events? She is beautiful, poised and educated. She comes from the right kind of family with prominent ties to the community and could easily converse with the powers that be. I know it's shallow to boil Claire down to the boxes she ticks, but I almost can't help it. Achieving goals is a habit hard to break.

A habit that makes it easier to ignore the pull of a new-age woman like Shay who somehow seems more real than the women I've dated.

"You'll find your Mr. Right." Thea gives me a knowing look over her shoulder. "Colin, why don't you walk Claire to her car?"

"Oh, that's not necessary," Claire replies.

"I insist." I open the front door, and Claire cocks her head to one side. I think she's going to disagree, but instead she gives Thea a quick hug and strolls past me. A whiff of her scent catches me: signature Claire.

Once we make it to her Lexus, she spins around to face me. "You didn't have to walk me out."

"And you never answered if we could meet up again."

"No, I didn't, but…why not catch up with an old friend?"

She recites her number, and I quickly reach inside the back pocket of my jeans to pull out my iPhone to dial it. When I do, her phone rings.

"That's my number. Use it." She glides inside her car and backs out of the driveway.

Did I really just get another chance with my dream girl?

When I walk back inside, I'm still in disbelief, but my joy is eclipsed when Thea promptly slaps me on the arm. "Not only were you late to meet your niece, but you missed your chance for dinner with Claire. I had it all teed up."

"I'm sorry, but it couldn't be avoided."

"Bullshit, Colin. You could have come earlier, or at least let us know your change of plans. You *chose* not to."

"Damn it, Thea. Today was huge for me. Getting a chance to mingle with the heads of my company doesn't come every day."

"And neither does seeing your niece grow up."

"Fair enough, but I'm making an effort. I did come tonight. Don't I get credit for that?"

"Whatever," she starts for the stairs and turns to me. "If you're really quiet, you can come and see your niece *sleep*."

"I'd love that, sis."

Several moments later, I'm staring down at my angelic niece with her beautiful cocoa skin, chubby cheeks and a head chock-full of curly hair, and an emotion I can't quite name fills me. Yearning for something as honest as a baby's peaceful sleep? Bittersweet longing for something real, something different from what I'm headed toward? I shake it away.

Now that Claire Watson is back in the picture, everything I want is within my grasp. The day was perfect. The talk with Dan, seeing Claire again, getting her number—it's all leading me to becoming the success my father always wanted.

When Monday arrives, I walk into the office on cloud nine, my bright future ahead of me. The director of accounting job is mine. Giving me a seat at the executive table.

The cherry on top: Claire Watson. *The one who got away* is suddenly back in the picture.

Although I wanted to call Claire last night, I didn't. I don't want to appear too eager, and I still have to get through this road show. The finish line is in sight. I bust my ass all day, making sure the CFO has everything he needs, skipping a sit-down lunch for a greasy cheeseburger, powering through the facts and figures to ensure everything tallies. Then I double- and triple-check my work. Nothing can go wrong.

Hours later, I realize it's past five o'clock. Between the myriad meetings and preparations, the day got away from me. Standing up, I stretch my legs, avoid looking at the screen and head toward the door when a pressure in my chest knocks the wind out of me. I fall to the floor, and that's when Matt comes running to my door. He has the office next to mine.

"Colin, are you okay?"

I shake my head and hold my chest because the pressure isn't like anything I've ever felt. A cold sweat breaks out on my forehead. "I don't know..."

"I'm calling an ambulance." Matt pulls his phone out of his suit pocket.

The next several minutes go by in a whirl of activity. Matt helps me off the floor and into a chair in my office. Several people surround us, all curious to see what's going on. I hate being the center of attention. At least, not like this. Feeling vulnerable, I ask Matt to close the door, but just as he's about to, two men in EMT uniforms arrive with a stretcher.

For Christ's sake! I don't need a fucking stretcher.

It's probably heartburn from the burger I ate earlier.

"Sir, do you have any pain in your chest, arms or back?" one them of asks.

"Has he passed out?" The other one looks at Matt.

"No, I haven't," I answer curtly. Why is everyone making such a big fuss over nothing? I'm thirty. There's nothing wrong with my ticker. It's not like I smoke or anything, though I may have high blood pressure. The doctor mentioned a few months back I should follow up with him for meds, but I've had too much on my plate to make time for a doctor's appointment.

"It's j-just p-pressure in my chest." I can barely get the words out.

"Sir, we're going to need to do an EKG of your heart and be sure you're not having a heart attack," the first EMT says. "If I can have everyone step back, please." He motions all the onlookers away from my office.

"I'll need you to unbutton your shirt and lie down on the floor."

Undoing the buttons, I move to the floor. Is this really happening in my office right before the IPO road show? *What must everyone think?* I can't worry about it, though, because the EMT is putting leads on my chest. He attaches six of them. One each on my collarbone and chest, and two on my hands and legs. Then he adds the electrodes. "Now, we're going to run the electrocardiogram. You shouldn't feel a thing."

The entire process takes a couple of minutes. Once the reading prints out, I notice the EMTs look at each other.

"What is it?" I ask.

"Sir, your EKG is cause for concern. We need to take you to the hospital, but first—" he glances at his partner, who hands him a packet "—I'd like you to take this tablet. It's called nitroglycerin."

I've heard of it before. "Isn't that for heart attacks?"

"Not necessarily," the EMT states. "We'll leave that diagnosis to the doctor, but it does appear you're in cardiac distress, and we'd like you take this tablet."

I glance at Matt who nods encouragingly. "All right, if you think that's best." Accepting the pill they offer, I place it under my tongue.

I'm scared as hell. It makes me think of the frightening call I received from my mother when my father passed out in the doorway of our family home. The ambulance came and took Dad to the hospital, and we assumed he was out of danger. Mom, Thea and I visited him in the hospital, teasing him about taking better care of himself, when all of sudden he clutched his chest again.

Just like me.

Is the same thing happening? Am I going to die?

There's so much more I want to do with my life. I don't have my promotion yet. I'm not married, and I don't have any children. Will I get to have those moments? Or is this it?

My fear doesn't lessen as they load me onto the stretcher in front of my colleagues. It's mortifying, seeing their sad and shocked expressions. Closing my eyes, I pray for it to all be over, but it isn't.

The drive to the hospital is thankfully short, but the multitude of tests and questions once I'm there aren't. After making me get undressed and wear one of those god-awful hospital gowns with my ass hanging out, I'm poked and prodded and so much blood is taken, I think they must be vampires.

I can't call my mother or Thea because they will flip out. My mother will think she's losing me like she lost Dad, and I won't put her through that. It's better I don't worry them over nothing. Because it has to be nothing. I've been eating out a lot recently and haven't seen the inside of a gym in months, which isn't my norm. In the past, working out was a stress-reliever, but there hasn't been time.

Morning comes and goes with nurses checking on me every couple of hours. How do they expect anyone to rest if they are constantly interrupting?

Hours later, a short brunette doctor with a nurse at her side taps on my door. "Hello, I'm Dr. Shepard," she says, walking in.

"What's wrong with me, doc?" I ask, sitting upright in the hospital bed. I'm exhausted. I haven't eaten anything in hours and just want to go home.

"I apologize for the delay," she replies, "We had to rule out a heart attack, which we have. You have angina, Mr. Anderson."

"What's that?"

"It's a type of chest pain that's caused by reduced blood flow to your heart. It can often be described as squeezing, pressure, tightness or even pain that can feel like a weight is lying on your chest."

I frown. "I don't understand. I'm not an old man. I'm thirty."

"Do you smoke?" she inquires.

"No."

"Have a family history of heart disease?" she persists.

My head lowers. "My father died from a heart attack three years ago." I thought losing him was the worst thing that could happen to me. I was wrong.

She nods and glances at my chart. "And how about you?"

I was warned to come in after those bad labs. "My doctor mentioned I should see him about some blood-pressure meds."

Her eyebrow quirks at that info. "And you didn't?"

I shake my head.

"I see." I feel her quiet censure.

"I was going to get around to it," I explain quickly. "It's just been very busy at work with the IPO."

"Sounds stressful."

"It has been, but once we're over the hump, it'll be business as usual."

Dr. Shepard pulls up a stool and scoots closer to me. "Listen to me, Mr. Anderson. Angina is a warning, letting you know your heart is overtaxed. You should heed it. Getting your health in order is of utmost importance right now. That means going to your doctor appointments, getting on high blood pressure or cholesterol meds, eating right and getting enough exercise. Which from the sounds of it, you haven't been doing."

"You don't understand—" I begin, but she interrupts me.

"If you don't change your lifestyle, Mr. Anderson, you won't make it to another birthday."

Her blunt and straight-to-the-point words get my attention. "Are you saying I could have a heart attack?"

"Possibly," she responds, "but you're young, and if you

change your lifestyle and behavior, you can turn this around. It's up to you. I've signed your release papers. Once you're dressed, you're free to go, but you'll need to wait for the nurses to bring you the prescription I want you to take immediately. Also, I highly suggest you schedule an appointment with your primary physician and get a cardiologist."

Once the nurse returns with my paperwork, I dress quickly and rush down the hall, the doctor's harsh words on a running loop in my head. If I don't eat right, exercise and reduce my stress, I'm headed for a one-way ticket to the grave.

Just like my father.

Five

SHAY

I can't wait to see the new baby. One of my former coworkers, Eve, just had a boy, and I'm at the hospital with the requisite balloons and the biggest teddy bear I could find to congratulate her and her husband. Carrying so much doesn't allow me to see the whole hallway in front of me, and I run into a hard chest.

"Watch where you're going!" a deep male voice grunts.

The tone sounds familiar. I pull the balloons aside and stare into Colin's dark eyes. What on earth? It's been over a decade and somehow we run into each other twice in one week? "I would say I'm sorry, but *you* ran into *me*."

Colin snorts. "Maybe if you weren't carrying the entire flower shop, you'd be able to see in front of you."

"What bug crawled up your ass?" I snap. "I'm here to congratulate a friend on the birth of her son. Balloons and a teddy bear are the norm."

"Bully for her."

He is an ass, but then I notice the tension around his eyes and how his mouth is set in a firm line. *Why is he here at the hospital?* "Is everything okay?"

"What would you care?" Colin responds. "It's not as if I'm your favorite person. You said I was a jerk."

Smiling, I laugh inwardly. I meant every word. Our current encounter is cementing that opinion. How did I ever have a crush on him? Back then, he'd been cute and smart. I liked that he didn't fall into the geek or athlete crowd; he was in a league all his own. My sixteen-year-old self needs a talking-to on her taste in men. Maybe even my twenty-nine-year-old self too because I've been daydreaming about Colin much too often. "You may not be, but you look a little..."

He frowned. "A little what?"

"Devastated." Because there's no other way to describe the haggard look on his face. He looks as if he lost his best friend. "You didn't lose anyone," I glance around, "did you?"

"Just myself," he mutters.

"What was that?"

He shakes his head. "Nothing. I've got to go." He pushes past me, leaving me to wonder what the hell is going on with him.

As I climb the stairs to the third floor, I rebound from the encounter with Colin, but it's not easy. There's a lump in my throat. My heart hammers in my chest, and my hands are clammy. I shuffle the balloons around to wipe the dampness against my jeans. The last time I was at the hospital, I miscarried, so being here is already a trigger. The short but emotional encounter with Colin somehow brings up everything I've been trying not to think about. If circumstances were different, I'd be a mom now. I stop midstep and swipe an errant tear from my cheek.

Pull it together, Shay. Take a deep, calming breath. You can do this. You have to. Eve isn't just an employee, she's a friend.

I knock on the door and when they yell 'enter,' I push through.

"Congratulations!" Smiling warmly, I take in the sight of Eve, her husband, Bill, and the baby wrapped in her arms. "I brought these for you." I place the stuffed teddy bear and balloons in the corner and step forward.

Eve has dark circles under her eyes. She looks tired, but she's smiling from ear to ear. A beautiful pink-skinned bald baby with blue eyes is looking up at me.

The knot in my throat lessens, and I force myself to speak. "He's beautiful. What's his name?"

"Brody."

"I like it. It's a strong name."

"Would you like to hold him?" Eve asks. "I just breastfed him, so he should be good for a while."

"Yeah, my son has a big appetite." Bill's chest puffs out proudly.

"I would love to hold him."

Bill makes room for me on the chair by Eve's side, and I sit down. I wasn't prepared to hold a baby today, but Eve is exhausted, and within seconds the warm bundle is given to me. When I glance down, Brody is fast asleep. I can't help it: I lift him to my nose and inhale that new baby smell.

It's everything.

Tears fill my eyes, and I blink them back. This moment isn't about me. It's about Eve and her baby. Leaning back in the chair, I quietly sing a lullaby Mama used to sing to me when I was a little girl.

Why couldn't I be blessed with my own baby? Kevin and I tried, but every month my period came, every month I got sadder and sadder. When we finally did get pregnant, I was so excited. But then, two months into the pregnancy, I started spotting. At the hospital, they told me I'd miscarried. I was heartbroken. So was Kevin, but he wasn't the one unable to carry a pregnancy, I was. That first miscarriage had been the beginning of the end of us.

"Shay, are you all right?" Eve asks.

When I glance up, Eve and Bill are staring at me. My cheeks are wet, and I wipe them quickly with the back of my hand.

"I'm sorry. I don't know what it is about babies, but they make me so emotional. Must be hormones or something."

They both laugh, and it eases the awkwardness in the room. I hand Brody back to his mother. "He's beautiful."

"Thank you," Eve says. "You remember when I said I would come back to work after he was born?"

Cocking my head to one side, I answer for her. "You've changed your mind, right? After one look at him, I'm not surprised."

She nods. "I thought I could do it, but he needs me." She looks down at her newborn.

"Yes, he does, and I absolutely don't blame you. I would do the same. I'm not a mother, but if I were, I would want to spend as much time with my baby as I could. Listen, I'm going to skedaddle, but I'll visit you and Brody again real soon." Leaning down, I give Eve a quick hug and rush out of the room.

Once I'm in the hall, I lean back against the wall and take in big gulps of air. Seeing the baby doesn't just affect me mentally, it physically hurts. I wanted to be a mom so badly. I have to learn how to pull myself together around babies, because Asia and Blake are having their own son soon, and I'm going to be the godmother. I'll put on my big-girl panties and be the best godmother I can be.

But for tonight, just for tonight, I'll feel sorry for myself.

Heading to my car still reeling from that hospital visit, I notice a lone figure sitting on the bench outside with his elbows on his knees and his hands clasped. What makes me stop, I don't know, but I do.

It's Colin. He's still here.

I was upstairs for at least a half hour, maybe forty-five minutes. *What is he still doing here? Why hasn't he gone home?*

Should I walk over, given our last few interactions haven't been great? However, our interaction in the hall makes me want to find out what happened. I'm a bleeding heart and am used to helping my clients and my mom—and now Colin.

Inhaling deeply, I stroll over to him. His features look as if they are carved in stone, and I can't help but notice that even in repose, his mouth is beautiful and sensual. Sitting beside him, I don't speak. He gives me a sideways glance, and my breath catches in my throat. His dark brown eyes hold mine captive until eventually his expression shifts and he looks away, but he still doesn't talk. We sit in silence for several minutes.

"I was supposed to call an Uber," Colin finally says, "but I don't know… After the news I got from the doctor today, I guess I'm in shock."

"What did they say?"

Colin drops his head in his hands, and his fingers begin to tremble. His body radiates tension. He's not okay. Whatever the doctor said was upsetting. So much so, he wasn't even looking where he was going earlier when he bumped into me. I don't know why I want to comfort him, but I react on instinct. Slowly, I reach out and rub his back. At first he flinches, but he doesn't pull away. Instead, he accepts my touch. Somehow this feels right. I move my hands in slow circles, up and down, like I used to do for Mama when she was having one of her episodes.

He lets out a ragged breath as if he were holding it all in. "I never thought I'd be in this position," he says. The despair in his voice shocks me.

Elaborate, I want to tell him, but I don't. If he wants to tell me more, he will.

"I guess you were right." He looks straight at me. I'm not prepared because his gaze is strong and steady. My hand drops to my side, and I feel the urge to move away. Then he shocks me by saying, "Why did you stop?"

"I…" I don't have an answer. I can't very well tell him he's making me nervous just by looking at me, that I feel mixed emotions every time I encounter him. Instead, I return my hand to his back, and he starts speaking again.

"I was told I need to slow down and take care of myself.

Otherwise, I'm going to end up back here." He glances my way again, and this time I hold his gaze. We stare at each other, and something passes between us. Something I don't want to identify, but it's there. "You can say *I told you so.*"

"What fun would that be?" I ask, somewhat huskily even though my chest is aching in empathy for him because whatever he experienced today is bad. I continue to run my hands up and down his back. "You would be expecting it."

"I wasn't expecting you to comfort me. We aren't friends, but here you are." This time a smile curves his lips, and I find I rather like it. It warms his entire face, making him appear less arrogant, less formidable.

"I'm used to comforting others." I'm not about to tell him about my mother and the years I took care of her. How I had to be the parent instead of the child when I was only a kid myself.

"Hmmm...so you have a story, but you don't want to share," he surmises correctly.

"We don't know each other like that."

He sits upright, and I brace myself for the old Colin to return. Quickly, I remove my hand from his back. The cold mask I've seen before settles over his features, and the bleak expression and rawness of the moment is gone. This Colin has his guard up. For just a moment, he let me see his vulnerable side, and now he probably regrets it. "You're an anomaly, Shay Davis, and I can't figure you out."

"I'm ordinary, like any other woman."

He snorts. "You're not ordinary, Shay. Not in the least." He pulls out his phone, and I can see he's searching his apps, probably for an Uber.

"If you want, I can drop you home."

His head turns to look at me. My offer surprises him as much as it does me. Why am I being kind to a man who treats me with such indifference?

Colin shocks me with his answer. "All right, I'll take you up on that. If you don't mind," he adds. "I'm not too keen on waiting for an Uber. It's been a long and trying forty-eight hours."

"Uh, sure." We rise to our feet, and I start walking toward the parking garage. Within two long strides—or is it more of a slow stroll?—Colin catches up to me, walking alongside me with his hands in his pockets. I swallow the giant lump in my throat and with shaky legs continue moving until we reach my Hyundai.

The remote unlocks the doors, and he climbs into the passenger seat. I grapple with the sight of all six feet of him in my vehicle. Colin fills up the entire car, and I find it hard to breathe because I can smell his masculine scent. The spicy fragrance trails its way into my nostrils, and I find myself taking a sideways glance at him. In profile, the ruggedness of his jaw draws my attention to his five-o'clock shadow.

Colin is nothing like the men I usually date in his button-up shirt, fancy trousers and polished Italian shoes. Usually, he reeks of self-confidence, but not today.

"Thanks for the ride," he says, buckling himself into the seat.

I start the engine. "You're welcome. Where to?"

He gives me his address, which I add to the GPS in my phone and put the car into Drive. Colin quietly sits beside me, somehow making me vividly aware of his presence. My brain is buzzing to know more about his hospital stay and why he agreed to be alone in the car with me. As he said, we aren't friends. But we aren't exactly enemies.

Are we frenemies?

It's good he's silent, because at least I don't have his unsettling gaze on me. I fiercely resent that despite my best attempts, whenever I meet his eyes, heat pools low in my pelvis. I am a straight woman after all, and he is a virile, good-looking man.

"How is the mother and baby?" Colin asks me.

My brows crunch in consternation. "Pardon?"

"You had balloons and a teddy bear," Colin responds as if I should know what he's talking about.

Dear God. After talking with him on the bench, I'd completely forgotten about Eve. "They're doing well."

"I'm missing my niece grow up," he suddenly replies. "I haven't spent time with her in months because I've been so consumed with work, but now..."

"How old is she?" I inquire.

"Three months."

Damn, that is bad. He hasn't seen his niece in nearly three months? Babies change so much, and he's missing out on all of it, but I can't tell him that. He already feels guilty about his absence and doesn't need me pouring salt in his wounds. I try for positivity. "That just means you're going to have make it up to her with lots of stuffed animals."

He chuckles, and it feels good. Better than us battling wills.

"Like the giant teddy bear you brought to the hospital?" he says. "That thing was enormous. The boy won't even touch it until he's two or three."

I shrug. "It's the thought that counts, Mr. Anderson."

"Touché."

"Are you always this upbeat about life?"

"Usually."

He turns toward me in the seat. "How do you do it? How do you keep a positive outlook when the world is falling down around you?"

Was that what happened to him? I want to ask, but the information needs to be freely given. Instead, I answer him. "I grew up not knowing what the next day would bring. Some days were good, some were bad, but you can't let it bring you down. You have to *choose* to be happy."

"Easier said than done," Colin replies.

What would it be like to dig beneath Colin's surface and find out what makes him tick?

The drive to his apartment ends much too quickly as I pull up to the curb of a twenty-story building. Of course he would live in a high-rise with a concierge while I live in a sprawling suburban apartment complex. We couldn't be more different. He's downtown, and I'm suburbia.

I put the car in Park and wait for him to get out, but he doesn't. He turns to me, and my eyes go to his mouth. His lower lip is slightly fuller than his top one, and I wonder how they would feel against mine. Being in this tight space with Colin is ramping up the carnal thoughts. Letting out a breath, I bite my lower lip to control my wicked mind.

"Shay." The way he says my name sends tiny flutters rippling over my body.

What on earth is wrong with me? This is Colin Anderson, who a few days ago told me he thought my life's work was mumbo jumbo. I refuse to think about him this way.

Colin surprises me by saying, "Thank you for tonight. I didn't anticipate today, or yesterday, turning out how they did. I was supposed to be getting ready for my company's IPO road show. Instead..." Once again, he stops as if he's afraid to say more, or maybe it's me he doesn't want to reveal his deepest, darkest secrets to. "I appreciate the drive home."

And to my utter shock, he caresses my cheek with his palm before unbuckling his seat belt and exiting the vehicle.

My mouth drops open. What just happened?

And why is my face still burning from his touch?

Six

COLIN

The next morning, I wake up with a splitting headache and dread about the day ahead.

Everything had been going my way. Now, the top executives will remember me being carried away in a stretcher, rather than our rapport on the golf course. Everyone at the office is probably gossiping and wondering what happened.

What am I supposed to say?

At thirty, I had a heart episode—not quite a heart attack, but angina so acute the EMTs felt it necessary to take me to the emergency room.

What must the higher-ups think? That I'm too weak and fragile to continue with the IPO? That the stress caused this cardiac event? Will they leave me here in San Antonio to *rest*?

I wouldn't blame them, because resting is exactly what I need to do, but I hate it. I've worked on this IPO for nearly a year. To be unable to see it to the finish line—it grates on my nerves. To be so close to achieving the level of success my father wanted for me and to fall short… It's defeating.

How did I let this happen?

My heart pounds in my chest like an African drumbeat.

You know how, my inner voice says.

Deep down, I know my health and general well-being suffered in my quest to climb the corporate ladder. I've always been driven, pushed to excel, and this IPO only fueled my ambition. Finances, mergers and acquisitions. That's what I'm good at.

But now, after putting everything into this project, I'm told to *relax*. Learn how to manage my stress. Eat right. Exercise. Blah blah blah.

It's bullshit!

Telling my mother looms in my future, but right now I have to get through today. How do I go into the office and hold my head up in front of all my colleagues?

A ton of texts and calls flooded my phone after the ambulance took me away. So many that I had to shut it off. I couldn't handle the concern while dealing with the echocardiogram and a multitude of other tests. But now I have to face the music.

Throwing off the covers, I fling my legs over the bed, sit upright, turn on my phone and wait. A barrage of texts, missed calls and emails come through. There are over two dozen.

What happened?

Are you okay?

Did you have a heart attack?

The most notable one is from the CEO Dan Myers. There is only one reason he would call.

Listening to this voice mail could signal the end of my career, but I have no choice. I hit the Speaker button.

Colin, I just heard about your heart attack. I had no idea you suffered from a heart condition. I don't know when you'll get this message, but I want you to know that the entire company is behind you and your speedy recovery. Effective immediately, we're putting you on paid medical leave. Please take all the time you need to get yourself healthy. We look forward to having you back at the Myers Group. In the meantime, don't worry about the IPO: you had everything teed up and we're ready to go. Thanks again for everything you've done to get us to the finish line, buddy. We're all rooting for you.

They are putting me on medical leave!

Damn.

Did I ask for leave? No. They are doing this to mitigate the potential fallout so close to the IPO. They can't very well reveal their number-one accountant suffered a heart episode. Who would want to invest in a company that works their people to death? Literally.

Lowering my head, I rub the back of my neck with my hands. All my hard work, up in smoke, and I'm powerless to stop it.

Flinging myself backward, I fall onto the pillows. Time off? Don't want it. I need my job. I need my promotion. I need the success I've been working toward since I was a boy. Instead, I'm being put on the back burner and told to take it easy. Get rest. Take a vacation. How can I do that when everything I've worked for is at risk?

Getting up to pace the floor of my two-bedroom condo makes me more anxious. I have to make changes. That was evident from yesterday's scare. But I thought I could eat right and go to the gym, maybe take some meds. I can do all of that and keep working. What I didn't expect was no longer having a job to go back to, at least not for the near future.

My career has been my world, especially the last year, and although that's not a good thing, it was just temporary. Until I got to the top.

I ignore that little voice reminding me how hard I've *always* worked, even before the IPO, reminding me how hard it might have been to stop, even once I was at the top.

I stop pacing and pull my hands down my face. All the time and effort I've put in: wasted. And what the hell am I supposed to do with all this free time?

The ER doctor advised me to see my primary physician and seek out a cardiologist. But first things first, I need to tell my mom and Thea what happened. They'll be upset I didn't contact them sooner, but this episode has felt surreal, as if I were watching it happen to someone else, not me.

What was even stranger was Shay Davis being at the hospital last night to comfort me. Her presence calmed me, soothing away the pain and self-recrimination for ending up in this position. The way she looked at me, with such wide eyes, lit a match inside. If I could have, I would have drowned in the comfort she offered. I would have kissed her in the front seat of her Sonata.

What is it about this woman that's got me so hot? I've

never had a problem controlling my physical attraction to anyone, but last night my gaze kept drifting to the press of her teeth against the soft fullness of her mouth. I wanted to bite her and see if she tasted as sweet as she looked.

Shaking my head, I huff out a breath. That is *not* happening. The only thing I need to do now is get healthy, get back in the game. When I'm done, I'll be back on top, back to the promotion I deserve, back to winning over Claire.

After a quick call, my primary doctor makes room in his schedule later this afternoon. Then, I call the human resources department to find out my options. She informs me that my medical leave is for ninety days. Ninety days! The IPO is in a couple of weeks and the Myer's Group will carry on without me. I try not to let the thought of the long, long days ahead get to me.

There's only one thing left to do to get back on top. Get myself fit and prove to the Myers Group I have what it takes to sit at the executive table. I'll join a gym, get a trainer, hire a nutritionist, whatever's necessary to win.

Whatever's necessary to rid myself of memories of one sexy yoga instructor.

Two hours later, my physician reads me the riot act for not having come to him sooner. "Colin, you're a smart man. You must have known this could end badly?"

"I wasn't thinking, doc." Once again, I rub my hands over my head as a migraine starts to form. "I was focused on my work, on getting ahead."

"What about your health, Colin?" Dr. Nelson says. "Your blood pressure is high, and your cholesterol is equally as bad.

You could stroke out, or worse. I can't stress enough what a close call you had the other night. The angina is your body's way of telling you you're in trouble and to take better care of yourself. Eat right. Get plenty of sleep. Exercise. And most of all, reduce the stress in your life."

"Well, that's easy. My job put me on medical leave for the next ninety days, so I have nothing but time."

"Excellent. Heed this warning, Colin, and take the advice I've given you." The doctor writes out a note on a prescription pad, rips it off and hands it to me. "Here's my recommendation for a cardiologist. He'll ensure nothing else is going on and monitor your condition. Given your family history with your father..."

"Don't finish that sentence, doc." He knows that's a sensitive topic and one I don't discuss. *Ever.*

I can't talk about losing Dad because the pain is still too difficult. We were very close. His death hit me hard, and I'm not sure I've ever fully recovered. If he were alive, I would be calling him to ask for advice about this situation, but I can't because he's gone.

"Fine. I just need you to understand the importance of the position you're in."

"I do."

Leaving Dr. Nelson's office, I'm dazed, unsure where to go. I sit in my car and try to wrap my head around everything. The last forty-eight hours are a blur. It's all too much. My life is spinning out of control, and I can't find anything to grab.

How did I get here? I'm used to knowing my daily schedule, but suddenly I have nothing but time. Time to figure out where I went wrong and to make corrections. There's so much I want to do with my life. Have a family someday. Marry the right woman. Have children. But I can't do any of it if I'm six feet under.

I have to make a change.

Do something drastic.

Otherwise, I could be here again, or worse—dead.

Turning on the ignition, I drive with no destination in mind. Eventually, I pull into the retail plaza for Shay's yoga studio. Somehow, my instincts led me here. Why? I'm not sure. I've never been into new-age mumbo jumbo. Yet, here I am.

I'm debating whether to go in when her car pulls in beside me.

Tap, tap.

Shay stands outside my door with her hands on her hips. She's in the same getup she wore the first time we met. No, correction: the top is different. This one is nothing short of hot with a capital *H*. It's some sort of lace-up, revealing the tantalizing swell of her cleavage.

I swallow hard.

She motions for me to lower the window, so I do. "Colin? What are you doing here?"

She has no idea I've asked myself the very same question, but something led me to her studio. "I need help!" I blurt out.

Her brow furrows as if she doesn't understand.

"You're all about health and fitness, right?" Rolling up the window, I turn off the engine and exit the vehicle.

Shay takes a step backward as if she doesn't want to be too close to me. I try not to think about why I'm intrigued by that when I notice the rest of her outfit. High-waisted leggings cling to her tiny waist. *Jesus, Colin, focus. Don't survey her body like you've never seen a woman before.*

"You know I am," she replies, "but what's it to you? You think yoga is new-age mumbo jumbo."

"Well, now is your chance to prove me wrong."

"I don't understand."

"Can we go inside?" My head inclines toward her studio.

"Um, s-sure, I guess," she says, and I fall in step behind her. The lace-up design continues down her back, leading all the way to her deliciously round ass. Some men are all about breasts, but I'm not one of them. I like something to hold onto when I ride a woman, and I could certainly hold Shay's ass in my hands and send us both straight to the stratosphere.

"After you," she says, opening her studio door.

"Are you closed?" I precede her inside and notice the place is empty. She locks the door behind us.

"I normally shut down at noon and resume classes around four when most people get off work. It allows me time to go home, run errands or take care of studio business. But you didn't come here to find out how I run the place. What do you want, Colin?"

I walk toward her and notice she tenses but doesn't back down. She lifts her chin defiantly. There is something happening between us. Chemistry. Why I have it with Shay is a complete mystery. I should be thinking about Claire and setting up that date. About getting back on top so I can make my dad proud.

Getting entangled with Shay is none of those things.

"I want your help." I draw closer to her, pulled in by the excitement I feel every time I go head-to-head with Shay.

An answering hunger fills her eyes, even though she attempts to hide it.

"Which entails?"

When we are inches apart and close enough for me to touch her, I reach for her hand and place it over my chest. "I'm having some heart issues, and according to my doctor I need to figure out how to get fit, eat healthy and in general destress my life." The feel of her hand on me has my heart rate ratcheting up.

"That's no small order," Shay replies with a warm smile.

Being this close to her allows me to fully appreciate her smooth toffee skin unmarred by makeup. She's a natural beauty with thick curly lashes and dark brown eyes and a determined chin—along with a luscious mouth I watch with hunger.

Her eyes flare when she notices, and the pulse at the base of her throat beats fast. She can feel whatever this is between us too.

It's alive.

She pulls her hand away from my chest.

"If anyone can help me, you can," I state in a rush.

"I'm not taking any private clients," Shay responds, turning away from me to flick on the lights. "Not when I'm about to expand the studio."

"When is that happening?" Following her allows me to enjoy the view of her ass.

"Soon."

"Meaning it hasn't happened yet. I can help with that, you know."

Her mouth purses when she turns to face me. "Oh, really?"

"Yes. I don't expect you to help me for free. In fact, I will make it worth your while." Circling her, I inhale her scent. It's feminine and sweet with a touch of citrus. It makes me think about her soft curves pressed against my hard angles.

"Why would you do that? I doubt you'd do it out of the goodness of your heart. So what's in it for you?"

"If I can show my doctor I'm in good health, he'll sign a release authorizing me to go back to work—that would go a long way in proving to my company that I'm fit to resume my upward path toward a promotion. But the first step is getting fit. I thought about hiring a trainer, but then I realized I didn't need to look far. You are one."

"I am, but perhaps you should delve a little deeper. Your health scare could be telling you that you need to consider another profession."

My eyes narrow. "That isn't going to happen, Shay. I'm coming to you to get fit and healthy, not for work advice."

She rolls her eyes. "And why would I help you? You don't even believe in yoga, meditation, Pilates or anything else I might offer here."

"I will if you deliver results. And you can deliver, can't you?" She's only inches away from me now, striking distance if I made a move to test this attraction. "Or are you all talk and no substance?"

Fire flashes in her eyes. "You have no idea what I'm capable of, Colin Anderson."

"Try me."

She shakes her head. "I don't have time for this." She spins and walk away.

"I'll offer you twenty-five thousand dollars," I announce

to her retreating figure. I have no idea why I blurt out such an outrageous sum, but it's not like I don't have the money. I've done quite well for myself. I invest my salary and have savings. I'm not good with numbers for nothing.

Shay looks at me suddenly as if I've lost my mind. "That's a lot of money."

"It is, but it comes with stipulations."

"Which are?"

"The first is you have ninety days."

"Ninety days?" Shay responds. "If you really want to get serious about your health I need at least six months."

"No. It's ninety days. That's the length of my medical leave, and that's when I need to show I'm ready to return to work."

"And the second, because I assume there's a second?"

"You'll be at my beck and call when I want you." I added the last requirement just to get a rise out of her, and it works. She glares at me, and I like it.

The electricity building between us snaps and crackles. I don't know when it will pop, but when it does, it will be a glorious thing.

Seven

SHAY

"At your beck and call? No way."

I scoot past him to get some breathing room. The extra cash might help expand my yoga studio, but I won't be beholden to anyone, especially Colin. During my marriage, Kevin was in charge and held the purse strings. Young and naive, I allowed him to take the lead. Why? Because I was looking for love and validation. Looking for someone to make me whole because my own father didn't love me.

But I had to make myself whole. After the divorce, I did just that.

Now look at me. I know my purpose.

I have my own studio that helps others achieve a healthier, happier life.

I'm the boss.

This man, who for the last fifteen minutes has invaded my personal space and got so close I could see the flecks in his dark eyes, knows what he's doing. He wants me on edge. For what purpose? Wasn't I kind to him the other night after his health scare?

The attraction between us is borderline ridiculous, given I'm not exactly sure I like the guy.

He surprises me by not taking no for an answer. Instead, he charges for me like a predatory cat, and I hold my breath waiting for him to pounce. He doesn't. He smiles.

"How about I sweeten the pot? I'll give you fifty thousand dollars to fix me up in ninety days."

Why did he have to go and say a thing like that? Fifty thousand dollars? Yes, he has money. I can tell from the expensive suits and shoes, the Rolex he wears and the Audi he drives, but I never imagined this much money in one go. The only time I've ever had that kind of cash was my inheritance from Aunt Helaine.

Think, Shay.

I spin away from him, desperate for a reason to say *no*. No, because Colin is only getting healthy so he can go back to work, which might ultimately kill him if he isn't careful. No, because I'm not sure I can take being around him. He watches me as if he can see into my head. Read my mind. It's unnerving.

Suddenly, his hands are on my shoulders turning me around to face him. Energized, my pulse races as I meet his gaze.

"Don't tell me you're afraid of a little challenge, Shay?"

Was he talking about fitness or something else? Because from the look in his eyes, I would bet my life he's having indecent thoughts about me—the same ones I'm having about him.

"I'm not afraid of a challenge, Colin," I respond, eager to wipe the smirk off his face. "I just don't think you can handle everything I dish out."

He laughs, releasing me. The rich, melodious sound sends illicit shivers down my spine. "Oh, I can take it, Shay." His face moves closer to mine, and I can swear he's going to kiss me, but instead, he says, "I won't just take it, I'll crush it."

I know in my bones it's a risk accepting his proposal, but fifty thousand dollars can do a lot. Allow me to take over next door and fold it into the studio without asking for a bank loan. Ensure the studio's success and get me to the sustainable income I seek.

"C'mon, Shay. Are you really going to look a gift horse in the mouth?"

The word *mouth* causes me to stare at his. My heart thumps in my chest, and when I glance up at him, there's something hot and intense shifting in the velvety darkness of his eyes.

"Don't look at me like that, Shay," he warns.

I blink rapidly. "Like what?"

"You know what." His voice is deep and rougher than before. He moves closer to me.

I'm not imagining it. Something swirls between us. What if I take a step and stand on my tippy-toes and kiss him? What would he do then? Would I kiss away his carefully constructed plans? Would he grip my waist and pull me so close our bodies are perfectly aligned? Would he push his tongue into my mouth and kiss me hard? A part of me wants to explore the hunger that's been building between us, even though we both act as if it isn't there.

If I did, what would happen next?

"What's it going to be?" Colin asks again, invading my daydream with his question.

This deal is a risk.

There's no doubt about it. I'm attracted to Colin, and I suspect he's attracted to me, but we're both grown adults. Surely we can keep our hands to ourselves? It's not like he's my type, anyway. I don't care for corporate, buttoned-down guys. At least not usually. I'll keep the relationship strictly professional and only instruct him during the allotted time and stick to his health and wellness. And get fifty thousand dollars for my future.

I extend my hand. "I accept your deal."

When his long, strong fingers close around mine, all the air in my lungs leaves. His skin is warm and his grip firm. Everything in me relaxes, even though my entire body hums with excitement. I stare up at him, searching his face, but Colin's expression is neutral.

Embarrassed by the feelings he evokes, I pull my hand away. "Good. It's settled, then. You can begin with today's class at four. It's a beginner's introduction class and shouldn't cause you too much anxiety. It'll be a good breathing and stretching exercise for you. Help you relieve some of your tension."

"I'm not tense."

You might not be, but I am.

"You didn't agree to being at my beck and call," he says with a grin. "The more I think about it, maybe our lessons should be private. I don't know the first thing—" he motions his hand around "—about all this yoga stuff. I would prefer you to teach me yourself."

I can't blame him. A lot of men are uneasy with learning something new, especially yoga, and he's right. He's forking out a lot of cash for my services. "I can arrange that. Let me check my schedule and get back to you."

"There's no time like the present," he glances down at his watch. "It's two o'clock. Didn't you say your next class is at four?"

Why did I tell him my schedule? This unexpected turn of events has me off my game. "I have a few things to do..."

"My bank can have an earnest deposit of twenty-five thousand dollars sent to you today so can we get started."

He is playing hardball. He wasn't kidding when he said he wants me at his beck and call.

I let out an audible sigh. "All right, you'll need to remove your shoes." In the meantime, I drop my purse in my office and remind myself he's just another client.

When I return, he's already lowering himself to the ground and removing his sneakers, which look more expensive than my entire outfit.

My preference would be to relocate to the private room, but no matter, this can work for today. I mute the lighting, adjust the air-conditioning and light a few candles in the main studio.

"What are you doing?" he asks, his eyes following my every move.

"Setting the mood."

"For what?" He laughs. "Isn't this just exercise?"

I shake my head in exasperation. "Are you here to criticize or to learn yoga?"

"Yoga, I suppose." Colin doesn't say it very convincingly, and I wonder if he knows what he's gotten himself into.

"Do you even have a yoga mat?" I inquire. "If not, I have one I can loan you, but you really should get one of your own. I can suggest some brands for you."

"Do I look like I own a yoga mat?" he asks defensively.

Closing my eyes, I count from one to ten. When I open them, I find Colin smiling at me. "I'm sorry," he says, "that was uncalled for. I would appreciate your help on a selection."

"Thank you. I'll be right back." I need a moment's reprieve to collect myself. He's too much. Or maybe it's been so long since I've been around a man I'm attracted to, I'm imagining scenarios.

He is being more than generous with the money he's paying me to be his personal trainer. I'm good at what I do, but it's not like I'm a celebrity or anything. He's hired me to do a job, which requires I get him in tip-top shape in ninety days—and push down any attraction I'm feeling. Balance and Elevate comes first.

I return with my hair tie, two bottles of water from my fridge and a couple of yoga mats. I can't help but notice how fit Colin appears, but I'll know his true fitness level once the session begins. He walks around in his socks checking out the simple touches I've added to make the studio more inviting.

Connecting my iPhone to the speaker system, soft tunes drift through the air. I shake out the mats, placing one vertically at the front of the room and the other farther back so Colin can see me. I set a water bottle next to him.

"Are you ready?" I ask, standing a safe distance away.

He nods and smirks as if he knows I'm keeping much-needed space between us. He's dangerous for my concentration.

"Why don't you come down to the floor, and we'll start in the cobbler's pose?"

"The what?" He raises an eyebrow as I sit cross-legged on the floor, but he follows my actions, albeit clumsily.

"Sit up nice and tall with a long spine. Draw your feet in as close to your body as feels comfortable." Colin does so easily. "Very good. Allow your shoulders to relax. Tuck your chin slightly to lengthen your neck. Close your eyes."

Glancing over at him, his eyes aren't closed. Instead, he's watching me intently.

"Bring your hands to your chest. Palms together in prayer. Bow your head and take some deep breaths in and out. Nice and slow, exhaling for several breaths." He executes the movements, so I continue. "Now place your palms faceup on your knees, lift your chest, open your eyes and open up your chest."

I mirror the movements. "Okay, we're going to move our hips in a circular motion, forward, backward and down." I perform the actions and find Colin's eyes glued to my hips. "Fingertips upward and take a big breath, exhale and relax when you're done."

It's hard to ignore his hungry looks, but I do, focusing on showing him some breathing and twisting techniques while seated. He's able to keep up with me, much to my surprise. It's only when we come to the tabletop position, and I ask him to get on his toes, that he wobbles, but he doesn't give up. He perseveres. "Take a breath, inhale up, exhale down." After a few more movements, we drop onto our bellies, round our spines and thrust upward so we can go to the plank position.

When I ask Colin to get into the downward-facing dog position, he struggles. I move from the center of the room and rise to my feet to help. "May I touch you?"

He glances up at me with a grin. "Sure."

Ignoring his pointed smile, from behind I pull his hips back and upward. "That's right, your heels go all the way back. Spread your fingertips. Take a deep breath in and a long breath out. Breathe."

Colin looks at me, causing him to lose focus and tumble to the ground. "Colin!" I yelp.

He turns to look at me on his side. "That's not as easy as it looks on television."

We both laugh as he sits upright. "It takes practice, but you can't give up."

"What is all this going to do for me?" Colin asks.

"It's a scientific fact that yoga improves strength, balance and flexibility."

"Did you read that in one of your fitness manuals?"

My eyes narrow. "No, Colin. I'm a certified fitness instructor and health coach, but if you're not going to take me or this—" I point back and forth between us "—seriously, then we can stop right now. I've built a business on yoga because it's proven to help with back pain, arthritis and heart health."

"Really?" He sounds surprised.

"Regular yoga reduces stress levels and body inflammation, which includes high blood pressure. Are you listening, or do you still want to make fun of what I do?"

He lowers his head. "I'm sorry. I apologize for minimizing how you make your living. I wouldn't want someone doing the same thing to me."

"Good, let's go." I quickly hop to my feet and extend a hand to help him up. When he grasps my palm and stands, electricity shoots through me and I meet his eyes. He felt it too, because it was impossible to miss. Beneath his lashes, his gaze turns smoky. That fluttering excitement I felt earlier returns. Before I have a chance to move, he circles his arm around my waist, drawing me into the length of his hard, masculine body.

He towers over me with his wide shoulders and bulging biceps. I feel the heat of him and oddly I don't pull away. I plant my palms against his chest and feel the hard planes of his pectorals. I suck in a deep breath, and when I do, I smell his exotic male scent. My mouth waters.

I blink up at him, and there's a devilish glint in his eye. Like he knows he shouldn't do what he's about to do, but he's going to anyway. And I'm not supposed to *want* him to do it, because the success of B&E is more important than anything else.

Yet I've fantasied about this man since I was a teenager. Would one kiss really be so bad? He could be a terrible kisser, and all this angst would have been for nothing.

His warm fingertips beneath my chin exert enough pressure, forcing me to lift my gaze to his.

Anticipation and excitement quiver inside me because he takes his time, toying with me until finally he lowers his head and presses his lips to mine.

Colin is kissing me.

We're kissing.

I don't push him away. Instead, when his lips part mine, deepening the kiss, every cell in my body goes on high alert. A needy moan escapes my lips.

Was that me?

Yes, it was. I'd forgotten how sexy kissing can be. How passionate. Because passion is exactly what this is. Colin's five-o'clock shadow scratches me just before his cool tongue glides against the seam of my lips. My insides melt as he thrusts inside my mouth urgently, as if hunger has been building inside him too. When he finally makes contact with my tongue, he gently caresses it, back and forth. It's heaven. He tastes spicy, with a hint of coffee, and I don't want it to end. He doesn't either, because I hear my mewls of pleasure along with his groans. I snake my arms around his back, and he levers me against him.

The tips of my breasts pucker from the contact with his hard chest and the unmistakable bulge against my pelvis. His kisses are so deep and hot, sparks sizzle inside me like a firecracker about to explode. He is a skillful kisser. He blots out the entire world, and I don't care.

Colin devours me, and I welcome his aggressive ardor. It's been too long since I've felt like this. Needed. Wanted. Desired. I love the taste of him. It's minty, spicy—much like the man himself. Our tongues slide and mate as if we could go on and on…

But a loud cough sounds from behind us.

"Ahem!" It's Maribeth, one of my instructors. "I'm sorry to interrupt. I came in early before class, but if now isn't a good time..." A blush rises on her pink cheeks.

Colin moves away from me as if burned, as if he hadn't thrust his tongue in my mouth. I'm disappointed, and I can't say whether it's because the kiss ended or he pulled away or I followed my urges in the first place.

"No, you didn't interrupt," I respond, lowering my head because I'm thoroughly embarrassed at being caught making out with Colin. "We were just finishing up, weren't we?" I pray he agrees. We both need a moment to cool off.

"Yeah," he nods. "We're done." He bends down to pick up his bottle of water. He screws off the top and drains it as if quenching an unquenchable thirst. Did I make him that way? He turns to me. "Walk me out?"

Maribeth smiles knowingly, and I follow Colin as he heads toward the door and picks up his sneakers. When we reach the exit, he says. "About that..."

I shake my head and shrug. "It was nothing."

He shakes his head. "That wasn't nothing. It—it was unexpected."

Hell yes, it was. But I can't mess this up. Colin wants to pay me a generous sum that will help my business. I remind myself—*again*—that B&E comes first. "Yes, it was, but it can't happen again."

"Agreed." He nods, and I wonder if he's feeling regret. "I need your help, and I wouldn't want anything to complicate that."

"I understand." And I do. The kiss was a mistake, but damn if it didn't feel good in the moment.

"Is two o'clock a good time for our sessions?"

"Yes, that's fine." There would be less chance of being interrupted. Is that why I'm allowing an early time? Because deep down I want to see what might happen next? "But first, I'd like to take a few days and come up with a fitness plan. Let's officially start next Monday with sessions every other day." It's a cop-out, but I need time to evaluate how best to proceed.

"Should we exchange numbers in case you change your mind?" he asks.

"I won't."

"Just in case."

Why is he so persistent about my number? I walk over to the counter and grab a business card from the holder. "My number's on there. You can reach me any time."

"Day or night?" he asks, with a smirk. "You are supposed to be at my beck and call."

I can't resist laughing out loud. "You're incorrigible, Colin."

"All right, I'll see you then." And within seconds, he's gone, and I exhale. My mind rewinds to that incendiary kiss. Had it continued, it probably would have destroyed me in the best possible way.

"Who was that hunk?" Maribeth asks from behind me.

I spin around to face her. "*That* was trouble."

Eight

COLIN

What the hell just happened in there? I scrub my hand over my face, annoyed at the slight tremor of my hand.

How did I end up kissing Shay?

Sitting in my car, I breathe in and out and try to gain my composure. It was a moment of madness that quickly turned into something more. We crossed the boundaries of instructor and client when my hands wrapped in those thick locs and I tugged Shay's head back to press my mouth to hers. Her lips were as warm and soft as I'd imagined them, and she smelled fantastic. A mix of her own unique scent and citrus.

A hunger I hadn't known existed made me draw Shay closer, boiling in this attraction that has simmered between us since the moment we reconnected. The kiss was passionate and all-consuming. It made me lose all shred of sanity.

I don't want to *want* Shay, but I do.

My instincts tell me to run from how she makes me feel. I don't want to think about how her lips were swollen from my kisses. Or the moans she made when I thrust my tongue deep inside the sweet haven of her mouth.

Drawing in another breath, I remind myself that Claire is the perfect woman, the one who will know how to behave in every circumstance. A woman who will complement my climb up the social ladder. Claire is the wife type, as my father always said. He liked Claire back then. They had fun; she fit in. And she's even more polished now.

As for Shay, her less-than-stellar background and new-age lifestyle doesn't fit the corporate image I want to portray. But more importantly, she's dangerous. When I'm with her, I lose control—like I did today. All I could think about was having Shay's soft, delectable lips on mine.

I shake my head.

This can't happen again. It won't.

Somehow, I must keep Shay in a separate box labeled *Do Not Open* so I can get what I came for—a healthy outcome so I can return to work *and* get the girl. Now that Claire and I have reconnected, it's only a matter of time before we end up together. If I believe in something and work toward the goal, sooner or later it will manifest.

As for the money, I hadn't intended to offer so much. But fifty thousand is nothing when it comes to ensuring a long life. Shay's hesitancy, however, made me realize the amount had to be something substantial, an amount to get her to say *yes*, because she isn't my biggest fan. At least, she wasn't. Now I know she has a soft spot for me.

When she mentioned wanting to expand her business, I

saw an opportunity for us to both get what we want. Why go to a gym and do things that may not benefit me in the long run? A trainer like Shay can teach me what to do and how to eat so I won't end up in this position again. Shay was just in the right place at the right time. With her help, I'll get in shape, reach my dreams of becoming a high-level executive at the Myers Group, get the girl I was always meant to be with and make my father proud.

Just no more kissing.

After running a few errands, I stop at my family home. It's time I fill Mom in on what's happened.

My confession will cause drama. My mother is high-strung, and hearing that her eldest had a near-miss heart attack won't sit well with her. She'll worry I'm following in Dad's footsteps, but I'm not. Yes, I made a misstep by not watching my health, but I will turn it around. I will become the leader I'm meant to be.

Turning off the ignition, I walk up the drive to the two-story Mediterranean-style home and use my key. "Mom, are you home?"

"Hey, honey." My mother, a beautiful brown-skinned woman, comes toward me wearing dark slacks and a tunic. Her hair is a chic pixie cut, and her makeup looks flawless. She must have just gotten home from work. She's a schoolteacher for the fifth grade. "Colin, what a surprise. Shouldn't you be at work?" She gives me a quick hug and looks at me expectantly.

"About that, Ma," I reply. "Let's go into the living room."

Her eyes grow wide with fear. "Why? Is everything all right?"

I give her a winning smile. "Humor me."

"Okay." She leads me into an expansive gathering room decorated in blues and grays, which overlooks a designer gourmet kitchen with all the bells and whistles. Quartz countertops. Shaker cabinets. A subzero fridge. A six-burner stove. We sit on the couch, and I grab both her hands.

Since Dad passed, I've noticed how fragile Mom is. Dad was such a strong personality, a force of nature, that sometimes Mom was relegated to the background. She was used to Dad handling the bills and any repairs. As her son and the eldest, I've taken on that more traditional role as the man of the house.

"I don't want you to freak out, Mom, but I was in the hospital a couple of days ago."

Her face contorts with shock. "You were? Why didn't you tell me?"

"Because I didn't want you to worry if it was nothing."

"Colin, any time you're in the hospital, I want to know about it." There's genuine hurt in her tone. "How could you keep something like this from me?"

"You're right. Afterward, I realized I should have contacted you because it could have been serious."

"But it wasn't?" she asks, picking up on what I'm not saying.

"I wouldn't say that. It was a health scare that's shown me I've put in too many hours at work, that stress isn't good for me. Add lack of exercise and no proper diet—it was a recipe for disaster."

"Oh my God, Colin. Are you okay?" She grasps both

sides of my face and looks me over as if she's checking for injuries.

"I'm fine, Mom," I say, removing her hands. I'm not a three-year-old boy with a boo-boo who needs his mother to kiss it and make it better.

My mom wrings her hands. "It's not okay. You could have died, and I wouldn't have known."

"Died?" Suddenly, Thea is standing in the doorway, a stunned expression on her features, holding Kira. "What's going on, Colin?"

I inhale deeply because I'll have to explain the entire thing over again. Except this time, Thea will want details. She's not going to accept a pat answer. Revealing the chest pain and angina is met with horror, so I don't tell them about being taken away by ambulance.

"This is serious Colin," Thea replies. "You didn't think you could tell us?"

"It's not that. I didn't know what was happening myself. I'm young and healthy, or so I thought. I had no idea of the gravity of the situation. But it's all under control. I've gone to see my primary physician and I'm taking medication for my high blood pressure and cholesterol. I even hired a personal trainer and nutritionist to make sure I'm on the straight and narrow."

"And work?" Thea presses. She knows how ambitious I am.

"I'm taking a medical leave of absence."

"Medical leave?" My mother clutches her chest. "Your condition must be more serious than you're telling us."

"No!" I shake my head furiously. "A medical leave is the

best thing for me, Ma," I respond, not wanting to go into the fact that it wasn't my choice to take one. "It will give me time to figure out how to deal with life's stresses."

"I'm worried, Colin." Fear is etched across my mama's face.

"It was a scare, but I'm okay. I'm taking the steps I need to get better."

My mother sighs. "That's good. It's just…the thought of anything to happening to you… You and Thea are my world."

"I'm sorry I gave you a fright, but I've got this. Let's not harp on it, okay? I'll keep you both updated on my progress."

"All right, but what does this mean for your future with the company?" my mother asks. "Your father and I have always seen you achieving great things."

I nod. My parents, Mom included, always pushed me to excel. "When I return, I'll be headed for a promotion. Nothing will change. I promise."

Mom sighs. "If you say so. What else is going on in your life?"

"You remember that girl I was seeing during my senior year and into college?"

"Her name was Claire, right?" my mom asks. "I always liked her. She was so poised and put-together. And her family was equally as nice."

"I'm glad because I'm hoping to reconnect with her."

"And pick up where they left off," Thea adds with a smile, bouncing Kira on her knee.

"Claire is someone you want?" my mother wisely inquires.

He wasn't sure how to answer that question except to point

out, "She was the one who got away. Dad always thought so. He saw Claire as wife material."

"We don't always get second chances, son," my mother replies. "I hope things are better the second time around."

"I hope so too."

After I leave my family, I think about a future with Claire. Like achieving any goal, there will be work involved. Get healthy and fit. Remove stress from my life. Learn to balance my responsibilities so I can have a personal life.

And yet I can't stop thinking about Shay—her soft, succulent lips, her locs down to her firm ass, the way I want to clutch her with both hands as I ram inside her.

I'm horny. That's all. It's been too long since I've taken care of my sexual needs because I was so focused on the IPO. All I need is a good fuck. It'll help ease the tension.

So why is the person I want to help me with my particular affliction the one woman I *shouldn't* want?

Nine

SHAY

"Do you think she's going to like it?"

Lyric and I fuss over last-minute arrangements for Wynter's bridal shower on Saturday.

When I originally found out Wynter and Riley were messing around, I was none too pleased. Actually, that's the understatement of the year: I was downright pissed because I didn't think my brother was ready for love, and Wynter deserves the best. But, lo and behold, he proved me wrong. He proposed, and their wedding is fast approaching.

Neither Lyric nor I had time to put the shower together, not with my busy yoga schedule and Lyric working as a dance teacher in Memphis while simultaneously getting her studio off the ground. We combined resources and drummed up enough moola to afford a party planner.

"She'll love it because *we* put it together," Lyric responds.

She looks beautiful with her auburn hair in an elaborate updo, wearing the perfect slip dress for her slender figure. Although she isn't a professional ballerina anymore, Lyric's natural grace is evident.

"Thanks, girlfriend." She's right. I'm putting too much pressure on us. Egypt and Teagan threw an amazing bachelorette party in Vegas, and I wanted to do something equally as elaborate. That's hard to do with champagne tastes and a beer budget. Yet somehow, Lyric and I managed this shindig at a beautiful teahouse in San Antonio with an outdoor terrace seating forty people.

Wynter gave us her guest list, which included the Six Gems, her mother and sister-in-law, Francesca, my mother, Eliza, and a few of her colleagues at the online travel magazine she started over a year ago.

Our theme for the shower is Bubbles and Besties. The party planner has the entire outdoor space decked out in rose gold. There's even a pink- and rose-gold-balloon backdrop where Wynter can take pictures with the shower guests.

A champagne table sits front and center with fruits and juices to make mimosas. The dessert table has a rose-gold-and-white cake, éclairs, cake pops and macarons, along with small champagne bottles of Moët & Chandon as party favors.

"How's the yoga studio?" Lyric asks as we step back and survey the teahouse.

Everything looks absolutely divine.

The table decor is set up with seasonal blooms that catch the eye. The buffet has the menu we selected: a charcuterie-board wall with each cone filled with local cheese, cured meats, olives and fresh fruits. Then there's caprese salad skewers, mac and cheese bites, mini quiches, lobster rolls, mini cucumber sandwiches and a variety of pasta salads.

"The studio is great," I reply. "Membership is steady, and after a year I'm finally seeing a small profit. I've even hired two-part time instructors."

"That's fabulous, but do you rest? Ever? Since I've known you, you're always on the go. First with your mom, then school and Kevin, and now the studio."

"Is there any other way to be? Besides, it keeps me occupied and not thinking about what I don't have."

"It isn't easy seeing everyone so happy, is it?" Lyric asks. "Even Asia snagged a fella, and she wasn't even trying."

I nod. "I want the very best for them, and I'm glad they've found love, but it gets lonely at times. That's why I work so much—a cure for loneliness."

"I get it. Don't you think I'm envious too? I want to find my person, but...maybe it just isn't our time."

"I know what time it is." A soprano voice trills from behind us. "It's Gem time!" We turn to see the loudmouth, and I'm not surprised it's Egypt. She's a take-me-as-I-am kind of woman, and that's never gonna change. She sashays onto the terrace like she owns the place in a black one-piece jumpsuit with a large gold chain belt, rocking some killer high-heeled sandals. I love how Egypt is unashamedly proud of her full figure. The jumpsuit shows off her voluptuous curves.

"Diva!" I yell, and we rush into each other's embrace.

When we finally pull apart, Egypt says, "Girl, what I wouldn't kill for your svelte figure. You are rocking that dress."

"Oh, this old thing." Egypt eyes me in my one-shoulder ruched blush bodycon dress. She has no idea I left the studio last night in a mad dash to find something suitable to wear. Sports bras, tank tops and yoga pants are my modus operandi. I rarely have an opportunity to get dressed up.

"You look good. As do you, Miss Lyric," Egypt gushes and gives Lyric an affectionate hug. "I've missed you girls."

"Can anyone else get in on the action?" I turn and see Teagan in her familiar short pixie-cut hairdo, her brown skin and makeup flawless as always. Surprisingly, though, she's not in a suit. The woman lives in them, but today she has on an elegant tangerine sheath.

"Of course you can get in on the action—" Before I can finish, a squeal of delight erupts, and Asia's petite figure squeezes into a group hug. Her round tummy is prominent now that she's in her second trimester. "Don't leave me out," she wails.

Soon, we're all in one big hug of friendship and sisterhood. It's how Wynter finds us when she walks in with her mother and sister-in-law.

"My five favorite ladies." Wynter bestows us with one of her signature smiles. "Shay and Lyric, thank you so much for all of this." She motions around the room with her hand. "It's absolutely perfect."

Lyric and I beam with pride. We don't come from money like Wynter, but we did our best to make the day special. I'm no socialite and certainly don't mix with the country-club set. Mrs. Barrington has never thought the Gems were good enough to associate with Wynter because we're not from affluent families.

I'm not a fan of Wynter's mother or her sister-in-law, but as the hostess for the event I walk over and greet them. "Welcome."

Mrs. Barrington is a sophisticated socialite with perfectly coiffed hair. She's wearing a draped jersey dress hitting right below the knee. "Thank you for having us, Shay. I have to admit I would never have pictured this venue. You always seem so bohemian, but this is perfect for my Wynter."

Of course she had to include an insult with her niceties. Francesca doesn't speak at all and walks away with Mrs. Barrington without acknowledging me.

"That woman is a viper," Egypt says from behind me. "Don't let her get to you."

"Oh, I won't," I respond. "This day is all about Wynter."

Soon my own family arrives. "Mama." I rush over and give her a hug and kiss. "Glad you could make it."

"I don't like crowds," Mama says, "but your brother reminded me this day is not only for the woman he loves, but you planned it too." She glances around the terrace. "And it looks incredible, honey." She gives my hand a gentle squeeze.

"Thanks, Mama." She's never done well in social gatherings of more than a handful of people, but today she made the effort. I'm so proud of her and excited she could attend,

"Thank you." I tell Riley, looking into his ebony eyes, "It's time for you to go. This isn't a coed kind of shower." He may tower over me, but that doesn't mean I can't boss him around. Usually, people can't tell we're related because his skin is chestnut brown while mine is the color of toffee.

His jet-black hair is closely cropped while I've been rocking my low-maintenance dark brown locs for several years.

He laughs. "You don't have to tell me twice. Garrett came with Egypt, and he's outside waiting for me. We're headed to the bar to watch some baseball."

"Sounds like a fabulous idea." After I push him toward the door, I head over to the Gems.

The bridal shower is a success. Everyone loves the food and the silly games like who knows the bride best, and most of all Wynter loves her gifts.

Eventually, the afternoon comes to an end, and it's just the Six Gems sitting around talking. Mrs. Barrington and Francesca's driver fetches them, and Riley picks up Mama and takes her back home.

"Shay, Lyric." Wynter looks at both of us from across the table. "Thank you for such a wonderful day. It was more than I could have hoped for."

"You deserve it," I respond. "There's no one else I would rather have marry into my family than another Gem."

Tears brook on Wynter's eyelids, and she rushes over to squeeze me into a hug.

"Ladies, I did not come here to cry." Teagan dabs at her eyes with a handkerchief. "I'm here to celebrate the one and only Wynter. Join me in a toast." She raises her champagne flute.

"To Wynter," we all say in unison and clink flutes.

"Now it's time to dish." Egypt leans back in her chair. "I want to know everything that's been going on, and don't think about giving me the edited version." She turns to me as if I'm the worst offender.

"Listen, you know what I've got going on. The yoga studio's doing great. So great I'm expanding."

"Kudos!" Teagan claps. "A woman who knows what she wants and goes after it."

"Damn right." I hop on the bandwagon. "My neighbor is closing, and I'll expand and add Pilates to the mix."

"That's fantastic," Egypt responds.

Looking across the table, I incline my head at Asia. "How's the pregnancy progressing?" She wasn't showing when we saw her in Vegas a few months ago, but now her baby bump is evident.

Asia pats her stomach. "If you had told me several months ago, I would be engaged and having a baby, I would have told you that you were crazy, but Blake is an amazing man. As for the baby, we had a hiccup, but it's been smooth sailing ever since."

Asia had a pregnancy scare recently, and I was concerned, but she appears to be in great health. In fact, she's radiant. "You look gorgeous."

Once again, I find myself envious of one of my best friends and sisters, wishing I had a baby of my own. But I refuse to wallow. *Not today.* I glance over at Egypt. "And you? How are you and Garrett?"

"As in love as ever," Egypt replies with a wink. "And we've set a date for the wedding. A year from the day we met."

"That's not too soon?" Teagan asks. She's always worried about Egypt falling in love with Garrett, who had amnesia when they met. But he's well now and in full control of his family's farm.

"Quite frankly, it's not soon enough," Egypt responds

good-naturedly. "Although I love all of this for you, Wynter," she says as she motions around the terrace, "I would be happy with Garrett, a preacher, my dad and the Gems. That's all need."

"Who knew you were so romantic?" Asia laughs. "I thought you were made of stronger stock, Egypt. Is Garrett making you weak at the knees?"

"Girl, Garrett wears me out," Egypt replies with a naughty grin, and her index finger flies to her mouth. "Sometimes I have to tell him *enough*. I have a restaurant to run."

"And how is Flame doing these days?" Wynter asks. She isn't offended by Egypt's comment about big weddings. That's what I love about the Gems. We can tell each other anything. Talk shit. But at the end of the day, we would kick anyone's ass who dares come against us.

"Flame is one of the top restaurants in Raleigh right now," Egypt responds. "There's was a great write-up the other day in the *Raleigh News & Observer*."

"Excellent," Wynter says. "And you, Lyric?" All eyes turn to our sweet redhead, the quiet one in our bunch. "Whatcha got cooking?"

Lyric shrugs. "Obviously I'm not on par with all of you. I mean, Teagan had her brokerage business ready to go even before she received Aunt Helaine's inheritance."

Teagan laughs. "You know me, girl. When I want something, nothing stands in my way. But you sound a little shaky. Is there anything we—" she glances to the rest of us "—can do to help?"

Lyric exhales audibly. "It's been difficult trying to drum up membership for the dance studio. Everyone is so set on going to the other studio in town where all the ballet dancers go. I'll have to branch out and offer other styles of dance to draw them in. Luckily, ballet isn't the only dance training I received."

"That's smart," Teagan replies. "Diversifying your offering is key. What other types of dance are you considering?"

"My focus will primarily be ballet, but I'm going to add tap, jazz and contemporary."

"Sounds great," I say. "It's exactly what I'm doing at B&E. We have different kinds of yoga, including meditation, and soon we'll add Pilates."

"If you need help with your business plans, let me know," Egypt says looking in Lyric's direction.

"Egypt helped with mine," Asia offers, "and now my Six Gems jewelry store is up and running."

"Thank you." Lyric raises her hands in a prayer.

"I take it that means no one special in your life?" Wynter asks Lyric.

"Not yet."

"Teagan?" Wynter looks at the most career-minded of the Gems.

"When would I have the time?" Teagan inquires. "Real estate is booming in Phoenix."

When Egypt looks my way, I shake my head. "Don't look at me. Just because the three of you have Riley, Garrett and Blake doesn't mean the rest of us need to find a Dream Guy."

"True. I'm just asking if you're still open to it," Wynter responds. "I mean after Kevin and all."

"Just because I have a divorce under my belt doesn't mean I don't believe in love. It just means Kevin wasn't my person. I'm much too busy with B&E to have time for a relationship or a man."

"And what about Colin?" Wynter presses.

The moment she says his name, heat suffuses my entire body at the memory of Colin's lips when they crushed mine. When I glance up, several curious pairs of eyes are on me. "What?"

"You still like him, don't you?" Teagan points a finger at me.

"Like?" I shake my head. "No, absolutely not. But lust? Maybe a little." I explain how Colin and I reconnected and how he's hired me to get him fit and healthy.

The ladies immediately bombard me with questions. "Wait! Wait!" My hand shoots up to stave them off. "Just because I want him means nothing."

"Is the feeling mutual?" Egypt inquires.

Recalling the way he touched my waist, the way his fingers splayed on my hips bringing me into close contact with his hardening body, makes me answer honestly. "Yes, but he's hired me as his fitness instructor."

"Who cares?" Teagan shrugs. "You're both adults."

"Yeah, go for it," Asia says and nods encouragingly.

I do want a night with Colin. I'd like to know what it's like to have him buried so deep inside me I don't know where he begins and I end. But's it never going to happen. We come from different worlds. He comes from an affluent family with ties to the community. I come from a broken home with an MIA father and a mother battling mental illness. Besides, I'm more comfortable in my yoga pants and a tank top than in fancy clothes like Colin wears.

That's what I keep telling myself once the party is over and the Gems depart with plans to meet up for the wedding.

There's no possibility of Colin and me ever being together.

Ten

SHAY

On Monday, I mentally put on my armor for my next session with Colin. When he showed up out of the blue the other day asking for help, I was ill-prepared. He looked hella sexy with his broad shoulders, wide chest, lean hips and sexy five-o'clock shadow surrounded by deliciously full lips. Lips I haven't stopped thinking about since he ravaged my senses with that volcanic kiss. I've been craving more ever since.

But I give myself a stern warning. There will be no funny business today. He's paying fifty thousand dollars for me to help him get in shape. So last night, while relaxing on the couch, I created a fitness regime and eating plan to help Colin reduce his stress and curb his bad habits. It's not going to be easy teaching an old dog new tricks.

In ninety days, I'll get Colin where he wants to be. He's going to push back, though he did remarkably well with basic yoga. I went light on him. Stretching and breathing is a mild workout, but there will come a day that I'll push him to do more advanced moves. His body might resist, but if anyone can get him to his goal, I can.

There are too many certifications behind my name to allow one uptight accountant to get the better of me, even if my womanly bits stand up at attention each time he comes into proximity.

He's hired me to do a job, and that's what I'm going to do.

My clothing today can't be considered risqué or suggestive. I have on a loose-fitting T-shirt over my sports bra accompanied by some wide-leg yoga pants. My appearance will nip in the bud any ideas Colin might have that I'm open to more advances. He got the wrong impression: that I wouldn't mind a physical relationship. My body may scream *Yes, take me against the wall, on the floor or wherever you want*, but my mind says *No way.*

There will be no more kisses.

I'm not the woman for him. He needs someone he can take to his corporate shindigs, not a new-age woman like me who's uneasy with high society. Wynter is the socialite with a wealthy family to back her up. All I have is my business and the love of Riley and Mama. It's not that I think Colin or Wynter are better than me: they're not. However, most of my teenage years were spent taking care of Mama. Sometimes, she never left the house, which meant I stayed at home too. It meant I didn't go to the parties the Gems attended, meet people. Mama needed me, and with Riley living his best life in college, it fell to me to take care of her during her lows.

And there were always lows.

Occasionally, Mama had highs. Once, when she was having a good day, she cleaned the house, did laundry and made dinner like she used to when my father was around. I really wanted to go a basketball game after school and see Colin play. She told me to go have fun. I sat with the Gems on the bleachers and cheered as Colin ran the ball down the court. Even though he ignored me, I loved acting like other teenagers my age. Sadly, those times were few and far between because of Mama's depressive episodes.

I'm taking care of my own needs now, and anything with Colin beyond fitness training can't be part of it.

"Shay?" Colin stands in the doorway of my office at the back of the studio. At my frown, he starts talking quickly. "I'm sorry, the front door was open. I assumed it was okay to come in. I called out, and when you didn't answer I came looking for you."

"It's fine," I say, unable to take my eyes off him. Today, he's in a NOBULL tank top and joggers that sculpt to his muscled thighs and legs. *Breathe, Shay. Breathe.* "Please have a seat." I motion to the chair in front of my desk. "I've come up with a meal plan. I'd like to go over it with you."

He raises a brow. "Let's hear it." He accepts the pages I hand him.

"The first is an overall plan of the items you can eat, such as lean proteins, vegetables and preferred fruits. The second is a sample menu. It's one of my go-tos for new clients."

His eyes skim over the pages, and then he looks at me. "Is this necessary? It's awfully restrictive."

"Didn't you tell me you have high blood pressure and

high cholesterol? We need to reduce your salt intake and watch out for fried and processed foods."

"I didn't realize how much of a lifestyle change this would be."

"It has to be if you want to see improvement in ninety days. I'd like to take you grocery shopping and make sure you're on the right path."

He smiles broadly. "That would great."

"The first step is nutrition. You can't out train your diet. You can exercise as much as you want, but it won't change your numbers if you're not eating right."

Colin nods. "I may not like it, but I understand."

"Glad you're on board." I rise to my feet. "Let's head to one of the smaller studios."

He stands and follows me to the room for private clients who prefer one-on-one instruction.

When we arrive, I already have our mats, two blocks and some bolsters laid out. I motion Colin to his mat so we can begin.

As he gets into the squat position, I find him staring at me. His intense gaze reached inside and kicking up her pulse. "What is it?"

"You're all business today."

My brow quirks. "That's how it has to be." He's referring to our heated encounter last week, which I'm doing my best to forget. I find him incredibly attractive and prickles of awareness surge through me when he's nearby. He is certainly tempting.

He stares at me for several beats, and his molten chocolate gaze radiates heat. I wonder if he's going to argue, but instead he capitulates. "Agreed."

"Today we're going to do some restorative yoga. Use your arms to lie down on the mat. Once you're on your back, grab your knees to your chest and start circling them to give yourself a bit of a back massage."

Colin is a novice, and I walk him through a series of steps and poses from child's pose to warrior to pyramid pose, but the desire between us feels tangible. I can almost taste it in the air.

"These seems relatively easy," Colin comments from the floor.

"I have to work you up to the harder stuff. Let's try another pose," I reply. "Against the wall. Take your mat and blanket and follow me."

Placing my folded blanket in the middle of my mat, I support my neck and lie down on my back with my legs against the wall. I lead him through the legs-up-the wall pose, which will stretch his hamstrings and the back of his neck. "I'd like you to scoot your butt as close to the wall as you can."

When Colin isn't close enough, I ask him, "Is it all right if I touch you?" He gives me a stare so hot I feel every single inch of it on my skin and I almost don't move, but I'm his instructor so I go behind him and use his shoulders to scooch him closer to the wall.

Touching him sears my fingertips, firing up little explosions of fireworks. *Focus Shay.* We don't quite make it where he needs to be on the wall. It's something he'll have to work on.

Returning to my adjacent mat, I show him the pose again. Once again, his eyes are on me as if he's looking right into my soul and wanting to possess my ever thought. I work on my posture. My legs are straight, and I notice his knees are slightly bent. "It's okay if you can't do it yet. You can put your legs into a squat position it will relieve any lower back pain."

"No. I want to try," he responds.

"We'll get there. Relax your shoulders, and let your arms lie loosely at your sides, with your palms faceup." We lie there for several moments, deep-breathing and doing thigh stretches, before I eventually fold my knees into my chest, roll to my side and push onto my hands and knees until I'm back in the standing position.

When I look down, Colin is struggling to get back up. Extending a hand, I help him to his feet. He holds my hand for a bit too long and a bubble of warmth spreads inside me. "Everything okay?"

"Feels as if all the blood is rushing to my legs."

"Perfectly natural. With time and practice the poses will come more naturally to you. You did really well today. If you give me a minute, we can head to the store. I just want to be sure my other instructor is here for the next class."

"Sure thing." I leave him in the private room to find Dawn. In creating the schedule, I made sure I could devote sufficient time to Colin and his meal plan.

Dawn is already in the studio setting up for the next class. When I head back to the private room, Colin has already rolled up the mats.

"Did you spray those off? I have to disinfect them before each client. It's a must."

"No. I'm sorry."

"It's fine. Give them to me." I take the mats from him. "I can do it later. Are you ready to go shopping?"

"I'm eager with anticipation," he says drolly.

"If you're not serious, we don't have to continue training." I swivel on my heel, but Colin is right behind me.

"It was a joke, Shay," he says when we make it to my office. "If we're going to spend a lot of time together, you'll need to lighten up. Not everything is a dig at you."

"I'm sorry. But I'm serious about what I do."

"I see that, and I told you I'm committed to the process."

"Good." I bend over to grab my purse out of the drawer and when I right myself, Colin's eyes are on my ass. "See something you like?"

His full lips curve into a wide smile. "Don't play with fire, Shay."

I roll my eyes, but despite my best intentions I sashay my hips as I precede him down the hall. It gives me a secret thrill knowing he's watching me.

When we reach my car, Colin scoffs in disdain. "You want me to get in that?" He acts as if my Hyundai is a deathtrap, but he rode in it that night at the hospital. How easily he forgets.

Colin shakes his head. "No way. We're going in my Audi." He turns to the vehicle beside mine.

Shrugging, I move to the passenger door. "Whatever. You have to take the groceries home anyway."

He clicks the fob, and I slide into one of the most luxurious vehicles I've ever been in. Even Wynter doesn't drive around in pimped-out wheels like this. The leather sports seats feel like silk, and you can't miss the detailed diamond stitching and large touch-screen display.

"Nice wheels," I comment, buckling myself in and admiring all the gadgets.

"Thanks," Colin says, pulling out of the parking space. "Where to?"

"Let's hit up Whole Foods."

"That store has overpriced food you can get anywhere."

"That may be so, but you could use all the organic foods you can get."

"If you say so." He puts the car in Drive and pulls away from the plaza.

"Oh, you're finally going to do what I say?" I rub my hands together with glee. "I'm going to like this. I'll have to think other activities."

"I could think of a few," Colin responds underneath his breath.

I don't take the bait. "For starters, you'll start taking brisk walks in the mornings. It's a great way to relax your mind and get in some cardio."

"Walking sucks. Can't we run?"

"At this point, I'd rather you start slow, a brisk two-mile walk can do wonders."

"I'm used to more activity than this, Shay."

"And how's that working out? Did you or did you not end up in the hospital because you weren't taking care of yourself?"

He's silent, and I sense he doesn't appreciate my words.

"You've given me ninety days, so in return you get a drill

sergeant who's going stay on your ass and make sure you eat right and exercise."

"You made your point."

After a tense ten-minute drive, we pull into Whole Foods. I'm not Colin's biggest fan, but I was hired to get him in shape, and that's exactly what I'm going to do. Fifty thousand dollars is a lot of money.

We exit the vehicle and once inside, I grab a shopping cart. "We're shopping the perimeter of the store, that's where all the nutritious foods are, like your fruits, vegetables and protein."

"Yes, ma'am." Colin gives me a salute, and I roll my eyes, but he follows me inside. We walk the produce section, and I comment that he should buy brussels sprouts, but he resists.

"I don't like them. I prefer broccoli."

"You haven't had *my* brussels sprouts," I say confidently and defiantly place a bag of the veggies in the shopping cart.

He glares at me.

"Mine are the bomb, roasted in the oven with a little bit of balsamic vinaigrette."

"I don't know, Shay. My mom boiled them, and they were hideous."

"Trust me. I got you, boo."

His mouth creases into a smile. *"Boo?"*

"I'm sorry. I was just..." Flirting. That's what I was doing. And I know better. Today, I told myself I would treat him strictly as a client, but I can't deny that while sitting in the car with his muscles on full display, I was flustered.

Colin touches my shoulder. "It's okay to joke around, Shay. We both need to loosen up. We're wound a little tight."

You can say that again.

"C'mon." I incline my head toward the fruit display. "Let's talk berries."

An hour later, the shopping cart is loaded with a variety of veggies from kale to brussels sprouts, blueberries, red and green apples, good healthy fats like avocados and almonds, high-protein carbs like beans, quinoa and black beans as well as eggs, chicken breasts, salmon and lean turkey.

Eventually, we make our way to the checkout lane. Colin isn't impressed with my food choices, but he's a good sport even when the bill rings up at an impressive three hundred dollars.

Eating right isn't cheap.

He takes the cart from me and rolls it out to the car, placing the brown paper bags in his trunk.

"Now what?" he says. "Are you going to cook for me too?"

"I hadn't thought about it. Are you asking me to do meal prep?"

"Wouldn't be a bad idea."

"That can be arranged. If you're willing to pay for the food, I'll cook for you. We can start next week."

"Why not right now?" Colin asks.

"I..." *Why is he always pushing me?*

Unfortunately, I can't think of pithy comeback because I blocked off the entire afternoon, but cook for him? Without time for me to build up more emotional armor? It's probably not a good idea given the sexual tension between us.

But since I can't think on my feet, Colin takes it as a sign of acquiescence. "Great! Hop in." He closes the trunk and moves to the driver's side while I stand there looking like a fool.

Eventually, I climb into the passenger seat. "I don't have any meal-prep containers." The excuse is lame, but it's the best I can come up with on short notice.

"No problem." His thick lips broaden into a grin, and he pulls out his iPhone. "I'll order them on Instacart, and they'll have it over to us in a jiffy."

Why is he so gung ho about this?

Can't he see I'm trying to get out of this predicament? I glance over at him, and there's a twinkle in his eye. A small zing of awareness shoots through me. He absolutely knows what he's doing.

"That's fine." Shrugging, I act as if I don't care, but I'm worried about being alone with Colin and what might happen if there's no one to stop me from climbing him like a tree.

"Good. What's your address?" he asks. "I assume you want to cook at your place where you have everything?"

"That would be best." Rattling off my address, he pulls away from the curb. My nerves skyrocket on the drive, and my sex clenches with anticipation. Lust sizzles through me. Nothing is going to happen tonight. I won't let it. I'll cook him a meal, and he'll go home, but deep down I know that's a lie because I suspect by the end of the night, Colin will end up deep inside me and I'll be screaming out his name.

Eleven

COLIN

Shay was surprised by my request for her to cook. She didn't expect me to throw down the gauntlet, but I have no impulse control right now, not when all afternoon she's tried to keep me at a distance. Treating me as if I don't affect her. How can she act like this current isn't flowing between us? I can't ignore it, and that pisses me off because once again I'm not in control of my actions around her. I wanted to push her buttons, but instead I pushed my own.

She thought I wouldn't notice she's not in her usual attire. The last couple of times I've seen her, Shay was in a skimpy sports bra showing off her lithe figure, from the swell of her breasts to her delicious butt in tight leggings and yoga pants. Today, however, she is covered up in a T-shirt that hits her butt and wide-leg pants.

Hands off is the message, but my dick isn't receiving it.

All I could think about when she bent over to place the groceries in my trunk was that I wanted to pull her soft body into my arms. Excitement brims at the prospect of finally being able to fulfill the fantasies I've had about her since we first reconnected. I'm ready to claim all the pleasure I know is waiting for us.

Glancing over at her, she's sitting with her legs closed tightly. Is her pussy tightening as she wonders what my next move will be? The evening can move slowly, but it will take its inevitable conclusion.

My mind warns me to keep my distance and focus on my plan: get healthy, get Claire and get back on top at the Myers Group. Giving in to this need to be with Shay is the definition of insanity, but she's gotten under my skin. I'll be on edge until we see where this attraction goes.

To relax her, I ask how long she's lived in the suburbs.

"Not long," she responds. "Moved in after my divorce. I didn't want to be too far away from my mama."

"Is she ill?" I inquire, curious to know more about Shay. She is an enigma. What makes her tick? Even as I think the question, I know I shouldn't be getting in too deep. Instead, I should call Claire, follow the plan, but right now I want to be exactly where I am.

She pauses. "She's had some challenges, and its easier if I'm closer."

I nod. "How long have you been divorced?"

"Four years."

"You guys got married pretty young."

"We did." She doesn't look at me, just stares out the window. "I was looking for love to validate me and make me whole when I needed to love myself first."

Her words are considered, and I wonder why she had such low self-esteem. She's straightforward, hardworking and ambitious—all qualities I respect. The gates are open when I pull into her complex. The apartments are luxurious with a pond and a fountain. We drive past the clubhouse and pool area until Shay directs me to a three-story stucco building with enclosed patios. I park my Audi and turn off the engine.

Shay is already climbing out as if her pants are on fire. We unload the trunk, and I follow her to her building. Her apartment is on the second floor, but instead of taking the elevator and the easy way, Shay opts for the stairs. We climb a flight with arms full of bags until we stop at her door. She punches several digits into a keypad and opens the door, allowing me to precede her.

Her place is nice with luxury vinyl flooring throughout the kitchen and living room and carpet in what seems to be the bedroom. We deposit the bags on the granite countertop. The kitchen is high-end with stainless-steel appliances, wood cabinets and track lighting. The living room houses a soft suede couch and recliner, a ceiling fan and a large-screen television on the wall leading out to the enclosed patio.

"Do you mind?" I incline my head.

"Go right ahead," she says, unpacking the groceries.

Unlocking the door to the screened-in patio, I notice her apartment has a view of the pond. There's a walking trail, and a few folks are out with their dogs. "Nice place," I comment when I walk back inside.

"Thanks. It serves its purpose." She's already done unpacking and is sorting the food.

"Any idea what's for dinner?" I didn't have much for lunch other than a quick salad, and I'm starving.

She surveys the counter. "I'm thinking something easy like shrimp Florentine with zoodles."

My brow rises in confusion. "What are zoodles?"

"They're vegetables made to look like noodles." She holds up a package. "You didn't notice I put these in your cart?"

"You put a lot of stuff in there I would never eat, so I stopped paying attention and just let you do what you do."

She laughs. "You do know you're going to have to learn how to cook?"

I shrug. "I don't cook. Or at least not more than the basics like eggs and stuff. Anyway, that's what I have you for." My mouth curves into my sexiest grin.

"I didn't plan on cooking tonight," she replies, opening her refrigerator and pulling out some garlic.

"You want me to stay on track, don't you?"

She rolls her eyes but doesn't comment. So I sit on one of the barstools at the counter and enjoy the view as she sets about making dinner. After washing her hands, she pulls the remaining ingredients from the fridge. Then she chops up the garlic and cleans the shrimp. Olive oil in the skillet is followed by the zoodles, onion and garlic, then she adds a pinch of salt.

When it's done, she transfers the zoodle mixture to a bowl and stirs the shrimp into the same skillet along with more garlic. Then, there's spinach, a dash of lemon juice, some red pepper flakes and a few more seasonings. The entire meal takes her under thirty minutes. I'm wowed she crafted something so delicious in a short span of time.

"When did you learn to cook?" I ask after she's made our plates and set mine in front of me.

She shrugs. "I don't know. I watched my older brother, Riley, cook, and when he left for college I didn't have much choice but to learn if I wanted to eat. C'mon, I have a dining table."

She changes the subject from her family, and I sense it's a taboo topic. I follow her to a round four-seater metal table with a stone top. After grabbing us both some silverware and bottled water, we dig into the meal.

"You're always asking me questions. What about you?" Shay asks. "Was your mom always slaving away in the kitchen?"

I shake my head. "Quite the opposite. She was a working mother and is a teacher for the San Antonio public schools. Thanks to her schedule, she was always able to be home after school."

"That's commendable. I give props to her. And your dad?"

Now here's a subject *I* don't want to talk about, so I keep it brief. "He passed away a few years ago. He owned his own car dealership."

Shay surprises me by touching my hand. "I'm so sorry." She's genuine, much like she was that night at the hospital, even though I'd been a jerk to her.

But I don't want her pity right now. *I want her.* I turn her hand in mine and inspect it. "Your hands are so small." I place our hands palm to palm.

Heat surges in my blood. I want to pull her in my lap,

but I resist. We haven't even finished our meal. I release her hand, and she quickly pulls it back and lowers her eyes to her plate.

"Do you have any siblings?" she inquires, continuing to eat her shrimp Florentine while taking small sips of water. Is she as thirsty as I am, but not for water?

I nod as I finish up the dish. It's quite good even without real noodles. "My baby sister, Thea. How about you?"

"Just Riley. He's marrying my best friend Wynter in six weeks."

"How do you feel about that?"

"Initially? Anger. Mostly at Riley."

"Why's that?"

"They became lovers first." My eyes drift to hers at the word *lovers*. "But then Wynter fell in love, and Riley pushed her away, which made me upset because he didn't want to commit."

"They're getting married, so he must have changed his mind."

She smiles, and it reaches her eyes. "Yes, he did, and I'm happy for them."

"And what about you, Shay? What do you want?" Lifting the water bottle to my lips, I take a sip, but my eyes hold hers. It's a loaded question. Will she pick up the gauntlet I've thrown down? Or will we keep tiptoeing around the sparks flying between us? Ever since that kiss, I haven't been able to get the taste of her out of my mind.

I'm ready for another.

Shay's face flushes, and the pronounced rise and fall of her breasts are noticeable. She wants me, but she's afraid to take what she wants. She rises to her feet with her plate in hand, and I follow suit.

"Let me." I take the plate from her hand, deliberately touching her. Her eyes dart to mine, and her lips part so invitingly that I throw out caution, put both plates down on the table and take her in my arms.

"Colin." Her voice is deliciously throaty. I want to hear her call out my name when I'm balls deep inside her. "Please..."

"Please, what? Don't kiss you? I'm sorry, Shay. I can't keep that promise because all I've thought about is kissing you again. Tell me you want this so I can make you come with my tongue."

Her answer is to press her mouth to mine. A savage growl escapes, and I return the kiss. I leave her no room for air, let alone thinking. I'm done with thinking. I just want to feel. The kiss is hot and damp and demanding. Intimate and passionate. It feels like a potent drug slithering through my brains. My lower half throbs as I slant my lips over hers this way then that.

My fingers move to her dark locs, and I hold her head still so I can have more. More of her. I increase the urgency, devouring her mouth until her lips fall open, allowing me entry. I lick and stroke her tongue, drowning myself in her. I gorge on her taste and her breathless gasps. She wraps her fingers around my neck, and I trail wet kisses to her jaw. When I reach the pulse at her neck, I suck until she moans.

Moving us backward, we fall against the couch with Shay on top. She sets her knees on both sides of my hips and straddles me. I didn't expect her to take the lead, but I want

Shay anyway I can get her. Her on top. Me on top. Doggy-style. It doesn't matter as long as I'm inside her by the end of the night.

She must want the same thing, because she asks, "Do you have condoms?"

Plural. As in, we're going to need more than one.

"Hell yeah."

Twelve

SHAY

The taste and feel of Colin sweep my senses. As much as I tried to resist him, the inevitable happens.

I should be pushing him away, not pulling him close. I promised myself I wouldn't give in to the tug of desire between us because it can't go anywhere. He probably wants a socialite from a wealthy family who's comfortable in the country-club scene. That's not me.

However, I can't deny the delicious way Colin makes me feel. Maybe we can have this one night and move on. Yes, one night. That's all I'll allow myself. Colin and I are going to have sex. No, correction: we're going to fuck. Based on the passion-filled looks he's given me all night, he's not interested in taking it nice and slow.

The first time will be fast and loud, *very loud*. It's been too long since I've had dick. I've only been with a couple of men since my divorce, afraid of putting myself out there. My career and building my business were priorities for the last year. I hope I won't embarrass myself with screaming when I climax.

His hands slide down to my buttocks and scoot me closer until my crotch is on the thick ridge of his dick, right where I want it most.

I revel in the hungry pull of his lips and the sense of deep connection that courses through me when his tongue brushes mine. Before I can react, his hands gather the hem of my T-shirt and pull it over my head, letting it float to the floor. My sports bra follows. Then I hear a harsh growl seconds before Colin's hot mouth captures my nipple. He sucks on it with such delicious pressure that I push my breasts forward so he can take them even deeper. My entire body ignites, fire liquefying me from the inside out.

I start rocking and thrusting my hips desperate for relief. My sex is damp, but Colin's hands halt my hips. He lifts his head long enough to tell me, "The only way you're coming is in my mouth or with my dick inside you."

"Then, let's take care of that."

Quickly, I hop to my feet. Then Colin is pushing my yoga pants down my thighs and legs until I step out of them. He pushes me backward against the couch, then crawls between my legs. Seconds later his hot tongue is on me.

"Ah, oooh…" I purr as pleasure shoots through me.

Colin wastes no time on the task at hand. He flattens his tongue and licks at my softness. Sure, I had fantasies about this, but nothing compares to the reality of Colin eating me out like I'm his favorite meal. I grip his head as he strokes my clit with quick, light strokes before switching his rhythm and going deeper with his tongue.

He looks up at me as he spreads my legs farther apart and adds a finger along with his tongue. I moan. He adds a second finger into my wet heat, and I let out a string of curses. The slick glide is addictive, and my back arches off the sofa.

"You're so responsive, Shay," he mutters. "I like it." His other hand reaches up to pinch my nipple as his tongue laps at me and his other fingers stroke me.

I gasp. I sob. I pant. "Colin, please..."

That only makes him more voracious. Suddenly his teeth scrape my clit and I scream. "Oh my God!"

I don't care that I'm probably bothering the neighbors because I've reached the peak, the highest of highs, where I haven't been in oh so long, at least not with a partner. When Colin hits the spot, I shatter, grinding myself against his face. He holds my thighs, and his fingers continue their assault, wringing every ounce of pleasure out of me until I'm a quivering mass of sensations on the couch. Flopping back, I'm hot and shivering and incapable of movement.

I see Colin standing to remove his clothes. His shirt is first. My hungry gaze trails over his body. I'm itching to feel his washboard stomach against my fingers, but when he drops his shorts and briefs in one fell swoop and I lay eyes on what he's been packing underneath the clothes, I damn near swoon.

Colin's full, thick length bobs out in front of him. My eyes lock on his dick. In the past, I've never been a big fan of giving head, but the velvety weight of him is beautiful, makes me want to give it a try, but Colin is pulling a packet of condoms out and sliding one over the fat head of his straining erection.

"I need to be inside you," Colin says. "But perhaps we should do this in your bedroom?"

I agree, hastily jumping to my feet, retreating to my bedroom down the hall and plopping down on the bed. Colin fixes me with a heavy stare, and then he's on top of me, spreading my thighs with his knees and entering me with one deep thrust. My pussy tightens around him, and he lets out a guttural groan.

"Fuck, Shay," he growls, moving in and out. I whimper like a little kitten denied a treat. I want him to give it to me. I wrap my legs around his waist, and he pounds into me until spots dance behind my eyes.

"Oh God!"

Tightening my muscles, I squeeze him, and he leans down to kiss me. I suck on his tongue, and he clutches my ass, tilting me at just the right angle so he can thrust again.

"Touch yourself," Colin orders, and when I hesitate, he licks the rim of my ear, teasing it gently. "Do it!"

I sneak my hand between our bodies and touch my clit, circling it. My legs start to shake not just from my fingers but from Colin fucking me like I've never been fucked before.

"That's right, Shay," he encourages me while pumping into me hard and fast. Our bodies are drenched in sweat. "Come for me."

I obey and let out a satisfied moan as my body constricts around his. Sparks flood my body. When he gives one final thrust, he groans as he too reaches orgasm.

Afterward, Colin pulls away and disposes of the condom, then returns to pull the covers over us.

"I hope you didn't think that was all," he says when my eyes start to close. "We have two condoms left, and the night is still young."

We crossed the line.

Keep this professional is what I promised myself, but I was wrong. I thought I could keep the passion we share at bay, but I was lying to myself. There's no way we can go back to an instructor–client dynamic. This is bigger than I imagined it would be. I should ask Colin to go, but I don't.

Sleeping with him once is not enough.

And just as he predicted, one time turns into more.

Colin stays the whole night, and we use the other two condoms. Once in bed again, and another time in the shower when we attempt to get clean. That's an epic failure because no sooner than we're under the taps than Colin has my legs wrapped around his shoulders and my back against the tile so he could feast on my pussy again as if he is hungry for seconds. His tongue darts in and out of my sex so fucking good pleasure zaps through me.

Colin knows exactly how to handle my body. And afterward, when I've barely caught my breath, he crashes his mouth over mine and turns me around so he can take me from behind. I never knew sex could be this good.

This addictive.

When the sun rises, I crawl out of bed quietly so as not to wake him and head for my Keurig machine. Our clothes are strewn across my living room in our haste to get naked and fuck each other's brains out.

Making a single cup of coffee, I add cream and sugar and take a tentative sip. But thoughts of explosive sex with Colin fill my mind. I've never felt so alive or so needy. The things I let Colin do to me… The things I did to him in return…

How I tasted him the same way he'd tasted me. Colin is so uptight; I wanted to make him completely lose control. First, I stroked his dick with a light touch, then with firmer quicker movements. He never took his eyes off mine as I flattened my tongue and licked my way up from the base of his erection to the tip. Tension ratcheted up, and his hips began to move. When I finally put his dick into my warm, waiting mouth and simultaneously fondled his balls with my hands, he let out a satisfied moan.

"That's right, Shay. Take all of me."

Pressing both my palms to his thighs, my head moved up and down. Colin closed his eyes. I suspected he was trying to keep it together, but I wasn't going to let him. I released him long enough to take a deep breath and then took him as far as my gag reflex would allow. I sucked him until he gripped my locs and pumped into my mouth hard and fast. The next thing I knew he was bucking, and the salty taste of him slid down my tongue and the back of my throat as he filled me.

Afterward, I licked my lips, and he said, "God, that was the sexiest thing I've ever seen." Then he grasped my hips and proceeded to return the favor. All I remember hearing is "You're so fucking wet" before he dipped his head. The soft mewling sounds I made still have me blushing. I was desperate for his mouth and his fingers, and he pumped them religiously until I screamed out his name.

"Good morning!" A deep masculine voice says from behind me.

Startled from my reverie, I turn and see Colin standing naked at the doorway of my bedroom, wiping sleep from his eyes. Regulating my breathing is difficult because it's obvious he's semihard. "Good morning."

"I didn't mean to scare you."

"Yeah, I don't have many overnight guests." Instantly, I wish I could take back my words. He doesn't need to know about my sex life or lack thereof.

He smiles and walks to the living room, picking up his clothes. "You mind if I shower again?"

I shake my head.

"Would you care to join me?" He raises his brows.

"The last time that didn't go so well."

He smirks. "I know. I was hoping for a repeat."

"I don't think we have any more condoms."

His smile turns into a frown. "That's too bad. I was looking forward to tasting you this morning, but if you would rather not…"

As if I could turn down that offer.

My pussy tightens, and before I can think about the wisdom of my actions, I throw off my robe right there on the kitchen floor and saunter naked toward him. Rising on my tippy-toes, my lips press into his, and his hand cups the back of my neck pulling me to him.

The morning starts off with another mind-blowing orgasm.

Thirteen

COLIN

Last night was a revelation.

As I make my way back to my apartment later that morning, I realize my fantasies didn't come close to the hottest, most incredible night of sex I've ever had in my life! This is an unexpected complication to my carefully laid plans. Get fit, date Claire and win the promotion. Those were my goals—they still are. Yet, I'm torn between wanting something or, rather, *someone* I shouldn't.

Shay is funny and honest, ambitious, hardworking and sexy. When I took one of her dark berry nipples in my mouth last night—tugging, licking and savoring it—I made her wet. Shay is an exciting lover and so responsive. My dick is still heavy, throbbing, waiting for the next moment I can be inside her.

Sweet Jesus! The way she tastes against my tongue is addicting. The moans and whimpers she makes when I hit *the* spot make me wild. I wouldn't have left her apartment today if we'd had more condoms. Three was not enough.

We went through those in quick succession, but that did allow for other play. And Shay, although she may not often have overnight guests, knew exactly how to suck me off to make me start speaking in tongues. I thought we could extinguish the flame burning between us and move on, but we only started the kindling. A fire rages between us, and I don't know when it will die out. All I know is I'm counting the days until we can do it again.

I hope sleeping together doesn't make her want to pull out of our agreement. Her expertise will help get me back in shape so I can return to work. Besides, she has to train me for at least a month and a half because I already parted ways with twenty-five thousand dollars right after our first class and that kiss.

Meanwhile, I'm keeping myself busy. Matt is meeting me for lunch. If this were a medical leave I'd taken by choice, I wouldn't be checking in, but since I was sidelined so suddenly, I'm desperate to find out what's going on at the office.

Wearing my usual work attire of pressed navy trousers and a button-up shirt, Ferragamo shoes and my Rolex, I meet Matt at an exclusive restaurant not far from the office. He's already there when I arrive.

"It's so good to see you," I say when Matt rises to his feet. He greets me with a handshake and pat on the back before we sit down.

"You too, Colin. You're looking better. And, dare I say it, rested and relaxed."

"Did I not look that way before?"

"Not even close," Matt responds with a chuckle. "Your brows were always crunched in consternation, and your lips were always stern."

"Damn." I frown. "I didn't realize I was that bad."

"We're all overworked, but some of us know when to dial it back and go home."

"And I don't?" I ask, but before he can respond, I interrupt. "I suppose you're right. I only know one way and that's the hard way. All in, you know?"

"I do. It's what makes you a great controller, but you must learn some balance," Matt says. "How's that going?"

"Would it surprise you to hear I've taken up yoga?"

Matt laughs. "No way. You? Do yoga? You're kidding, right?"

I shake my head. "Nope. I have a personal instructor who's helping me get fit over the next ninety days. You know, the whole mind, body and spirit thing. Shay's really into wellness."

"Oh, I get it." Matt nods his head.

"You get what?"

"This whole get-fit thing is about a woman."

Yes, I want to win Claire back and get the promotion I so richly deserve, but I'm not willing to share that with Matt. We've developed a friendship over the years, but our relationship isn't so deep that I want to tell him my innermost thoughts.

"No, not at all." My jaw is firm. "I heard what the doctor said the night of the angina attack. She told me I need to make some lifestyle changes. So in addition to the yoga, Shay handles my meal prep to ensure I get a balanced diet."

"Sounds promising, Colin. It really does, but when you speak about Shay," he raises his brows for emphasis, "your eyes light up. Is something going on between you two?"

My mind goes to Shay with her ass up as I took her from behind. "We're…" I start, but I'm unable to finish.

"You're fucking her, aren't you?" Matt asks.

I lower my head. I can't lie even if I wanted to. The night is fresh in my memory. "It's a recent development."

"How recent?"

"As in, last night."

"And you're here with me?" Matt says. "And not getting busy?"

"First off, Shay owns her own yoga studio. She can't spend the entire day in bed with me just because I'm on leave. Besides, we ran out of condoms."

Matt's face turns red. "It was that good, huh?"

"I don't want to kiss and tell." I respect Shay too much for that.

"All right. Do you think this could get serious?"

"Nah, man. It's just sex. Nothing more."

"Does she know that?" Matt asks. "I've learned you need to be clear with a sexual partner from the outset about what the situationship is."

"Did you really just speak some slang?"

"Yeah." He laughs. "Very badly. But you get what I'm saying."

"I do. And I plan on having a conversation with Shay about the nature of our relationship. I don't want her to get any notions that we'll end up like her best friend and her brother who are getting married. My interest is her fitness skills, in and out of the bedroom." I take a breath, ready to change the subject. "Tell me about work."

"Everything is going great. The road show was a success. All the figures were perfect, but we knew they would be."

"That's great. When will the IPO open?"

"In a couple of weeks," Matt responds. "I'm excited to go to the New York Stock Exchange. Craig and Dan are great to work with."

Surprise crosses my features. "I thought only senior-level personnel would attend the event at the stock exchange?" Someone like me. Now Matt is going in my place?

"With you on leave, I was the next logical choice," Matt explains.

The logic make sense but also makes me wonder what's going on behind the scenes at the Myers Group. Should I be worried about my job? Matt and I have always had a friendly competition, but he could never outmatch me because I was there running the show. But without me on site, is my promotion in jeopardy?

Fourteen

SHAY

My body is still throbbing hours after Colin had his way with me in the shower. I never expected him to sit me on his face while his tongue did wicked things. Those areas haven't seen much action in the last couple of years so I'm feeling a bit sensitive.

"Have a good afternoon." I wave to several clients as they exit the studio.

My eleven-o'clock class is over, and I'm done for the day. Since my session with Colin isn't until tomorrow, I can take the time to regroup and figure out how to handle the reality of sex with Colin.

Colin!

How did I get here? I haven't seen Colin in years, yet we have this insane physical connection.

When he pushed me for dinner after we shared that incredible kiss, I knew our fates were sealed.

But now what?

We didn't talk last night.

There had only been screams, moans and groans as we fulfilled our fantasies.

In the cold light of day, I have to remember Colin has paid me to do a job. Twenty-five thousand dollars has already been added to my account. The money will jump-start the Pilates expansion. It just seems too good to be true. First, Aunt Helaine's generous gift, and now a man I hardly know, yet have crushed on for years, is paying me an enormous sum while fucking me every which way from Sunday?

How do I make sense of it all? One person knows exactly how things can change in an instant.

I FaceTime Asia because I have to talk to someone after last night's turn of events. Wynter is knee-deep in wedding stuff. Egypt will be prepping for dinner service, but Asia loves to dish.

"Hey, sunshine," Asia says with a smile when she answers. "What's up?"

"Girl..." A sigh escapes, and Asia tells Blake in the background she needs to take this call in the other room.

"Where are you?"

"I'm at Blake's. I've been spending nights here."

My mouth forms an O. I wasn't the biggest fan of their relationship when she told me he wanted to marry her. I cautioned her to be careful, not to rush things. Now look at me. Pot calling the kettle black.

"Don't judge, Shay. It's not like I'm sleeping around. He's my baby's father."

"I'm not judging you, Asia. I'm commiserating because I've found myself in your shoes."

"What?" Her brows furrow. "I don't understand."

"I slept with Colin."

"Where? When?" Asia blurts out dramatically.

I can't help but laugh. "At my place. Last night. We've been circling each other for weeks, the desire has been building. and last night it combusted."

"Oooh." Asia smiles knowingly. "How low did you go, Shay?"

"All the way, girlfriend. Quite honestly, it was the best sex of my life."

"Get out! With Colin?" Her voice rises an octave. "Do you think this has anything to do with your crush from all those years ago? You know, love unrequited and all that shit?"

"No, this was all about fucking."

"Shay!" Asia places a hand over her mouth. "I can't believe you're being so crass."

"C'mon. Aren't you the one who told me I need to scratch that particular itch?"

"Yes, I did. And from the wide smile on your face, can I assume there will be a repeat performance?"

"That's the question of the day," I respond. "Most of the time we argue and fuss at each other. We're more like frenemies."

"Could be your love language. 'Cause making up is always the fun part." Asia winks.

"Yeah, I wish I knew what he was thinking. I didn't intend for last night to happen, but now that it has, what's next? B&E is everything to me. I don't want to take my eyes off my goal, which is making the studio a success."

"Are you open to more?"

"Not really. I mean, we don't even *like* each other. We're frenemies who fuck. My divorce did a number on my head, and I don't know when or if I'll ever be ready for a relationship."

"Talk to the man, and once you do, call me. I'm just so happy you broke your two-year drought. Your pussy was about to shrivel up and die."

I burst out laughing. "Sometimes I can't with you, Asia. Good-bye."

"Have fun." She waves and hangs up.

Asia is right. I have to clarify what Colin and I are doing. The kiss opened Pandora's box, and now that we've had sex, I don't think we can close the lid.

I stop by to see Mama on the way home. I try to check in on her every few days, and maybe today it's a bit about avoiding going home. Because then, I'll have to remember what took place there.

Before I left, I put the sheets in the washer to rid them of Colin's smell—as if that were possible. He imprinted on my mind with all the ways he pleased me and vice versa. Despite all that, he hasn't called or texted me. Not sure how I feel about that.

When you have sex three times and give each other oral pleasure countless times, I dunno, I think that warrants *something.* But I haven't called or texted him either so…

Going to Mama's is a distraction. On my way there, I grab some dinner from Fresh Market that we can share.

The house is empty, and I glance down at my watch. It's only five thirty. Usually, she's home by now unless she has plans with Randy Carter, an older gentleman she's been dating the last couple of years. Seeing her happy and having companionship again is a wonderful thing.

I place my take-out bags on the counter, and that's when I hear music playing outside. Should've guessed. Mama is in her favorite place, the garden in the backyard with its tranquil koi pond. She's on her hands and knees, pulling weeds. "Hey, Mama."

"I'm sorry. I didn't hear you come in, baby doll." Mama rises to her feet and leans over to give me a quick peck on the cheek. "What brings you by?"

"Thought we could have dinner, if you're free?"

She smiles. "I would love that, Shay, but is this dinner or a wellness check?"

"Can it be both?" I hedge.

"As you can see," she motions downward, "I'm doing fine. Great, in fact. Both my children are happy and healthy. And so am I. I'm taking my antidepressants and able to get out of bed, wash my hair and eat. Plus, I have a beautiful home." She sweeps her arms to the garden, koi pond and built-in fire pit surrounded by Adirondack chairs. "I even have a beau who likes to take me out every now and then. What more can I ask for?"

"Not much more. But have you ever wanted more, Mama? Like getting married again?"

"Sometimes." She follows me as I make my way to one

of the chairs and we sit together. "Randy and I get along so well, but then I remember how devastated I was after your father ended things. I was no good to you or Riley. Yet your father still left you here with me. I suppose he thought I needed you more."

"Or he was a selfish asshole who was only thinking about himself. He's never once looked back, Mama. He remarried and made a new life without us. He doesn't even call us."

"And you're angry with him?"

I nod and wipe away an errant tear that somehow found its way down my cheek. "Of course I am. He deserted Riley and me. No offense, but he left us even knowing you weren't always in your right state of mind."

"And you're angry with me too?" Mama asks. "Because, in a way, I abandoned you too. To my own pain and sorrow. I couldn't deal with your father's affairs. When he finally left, it broke me. Broke a piece of my soul. But I have learned to move on. To be strong for me and for my children."

Reaching across for her hand, I give it a gentle squeeze. "I'd be lying if I said I wasn't angry with you for not taking better care of yourself and getting help. You allowed our father to define who you are and your self-worth. I won't ever do that when it comes to a man."

"You don't know what it's like to be in my shoes. And I certainly don't think you've known that kind of love before. The kind you would do anything for."

I frown. "I was married to Kevin."

She turns and looks at me. "But did you love him? Like, with all your soul? Did he make your heart go pitter-pat when you were together? If he did, I never saw it."

"When you put it like that, no. I've always been afraid of loving like that. Maybe I even held back a part of myself because I was afraid of getting hurt."

"When the time comes, you'll know that kind of love because the intensity will sweep you off your feet and you'll be powerless to resist."

Mama's words resonate inside me all through dinner and on the way home. I've never felt that kind of all-consuming love, the kind Wynter and Egypt talk about, the kind I suspect Asia is feeling. I loved my ex-husband in my own way, but probably not like I should have. I used him to cauterize the pain from being abandoned by nearly everyone in my life, from my father to my mother, even my own brother.

They all let me down in some fashion, and I've learned not to let many people get close, except the Gems. But then loving my girls is a different kind of love.

Deep in thought, I start climbing the landing to my second-floor apartment and find Colin sitting on the steps waiting for me.

"Colin?"

His lips stretch into a breathtaking smile, displaying his beautifully straight teeth. He stands and I get a good look at him. Today, he's casually dressed in a pair of navy blue slacks and a button-up shirt.

"I'm sorry for coming by unannounced."

I don't respond. Instead I move toward my door and punch in the code. When I hear the click, I don't open it right away because I have something on my mind.

"Are you?" I ask, glancing behind me. "Sorry, that is?"

His eyes narrow. "You're upset with me."

"It's been a long day, Colin. What do you want?"

"Can we go in and talk?"

That's not a good idea. If I let him inside my apartment, I know what's going to happen. A night of multiple orgasms. I want that…and I don't.

When I just fold my arms across my chest without budging, he stares back at me and sighs. "I'm sorry, Shay. I should have called, but I—"

"You what?"

"Last night took me by surprise, and I didn't know what to say." He walks toward me, and I find myself pushed against my front door as he comes closer, inches away from my lips.

Please don't kiss me. Please do *kiss me.*

If he does, I'll be weak and let him seduce me.

"Shay." He presses his forehead to mine, brings both hands to my face and looks at me intently. "Tell me I'm not the only one feeling this passion. Tell me you feel it as much as I do."

He's not alone.

There are sparks shimmering between us, threatening to burst into flame from just looking at each other, but I'm afraid of what Colin does to me. He could get too close, too deep, and strip away every sense of myself—like my father did to my mother. And yet I can't seem to resist him either.

When his thumbs go to my lips and rub across them, I'm robbed of speech.

Be strong, Shay.

Don't give in.

"I want to kiss you so badly. But only if you want me to."

Hell yes, I want him to.

Without thinking of the consequences, I grab his shirt

and pull him into me. Our mouths meet, and our tongues tangle in a flurry of movements that make me moan.

God, why does this man do it for me? I should be kicking him to the curb, but instead he's reaching for the door lever behind me and backing me into my apartment until I'm up against the living room wall. Then he slams the door shut as his tongue duels with mine. I sway closer as our tongues glide together. The pleasure he unleashes is sublime, and every cell in my body hungers for more.

Some small part of my brain is still working, alerting me that I have to stop this.

We need to talk. Clear the air.

I need to know what he wants from me. What the parameters are before this goes too far.

Pulling back, I press my fingers against his throbbing lips. "I agree we have incredible chemistry."

"Why do I feel there's a *but* coming?" he asks, looking at me with lust-filled eyes. From the bulge in his pants, I know he wants me.

"I need to know what this is. Or what it means."

"It means I want you in that bed," he says and points to my bedroom, "ass up."

He clearly knows what he wants, but that's not an answer. "Don't act dense, Colin. You know what I mean."

A smirk crosses his mouth. "Of course I do. You're asking where this connection is going? Here's the honest truth. I want to enjoy you, enjoy this." He motions back and forth between us. "I'm not looking for anything serious. Are you?"

I shake my head. All I want him to do is rip off my clothes and bend me over the couch.

"Good. We're in agreement," he continues. "My goal is to get fit and healthy so I can resume climbing the corporate ladder. But I have to learn how to balance my personal life, which I'm not very good at. I'm hoping you can teach me."

My shoulders hunch over. "You still want me to be your trainer?"

"Of course."

"Sex complicates things. Wouldn't it be better if we chalk up last night to a one-time thing and move on? I can help you better if we're platonic. It would be easier."

"I doubt that. We've been dancing around each other for weeks. Plus, I don't want *easy*." Colin moves toward me with precision until once again I find myself between his hard body and the wall. "I like things hard." And to prove it, he pushes the ridge of his erection into me, and I groan as he grinds against me.

"Colin, this isn't—" Words cease because he's kissing his way to the base of my throat and then over my neck and up to tease my ear. He bites down on my earlobe and then soothes the sting with his tongue. "So we're just f-f-friends with benefits?"

"Uh-huh. We're fuck buddies," Colin returns, "because I intend to fuck the hell out of you all night long."

My breath hisses between my teeth.

"And I came prepared." He moves away and produces a long length of condoms from his pocket.

"You felt that sure of yourself, huh? You didn't know I'd agree to this…this unorthodox arrangement."

"No, but I hoped. Imagine how much fun we'll have,

Shay. You can't tell me you weren't thinking about last night all day, because I know I was."

"You were?" I'm surprised he's willing to admit that out loud.

"Let's see where this goes. When one or both of us decides it's enough, we part ways. How does that sound?"

"What if we aren't done training?"

"Do you think we'll tire of each other that quickly?" he asks. "Because I'm certain I haven't found all the ways to please you and make you lose control."

My eyes widen. "I don't know."

Colin is overwhelming, but when have I ever felt an attraction like this before? Never, that's when. He makes my heart go pitter-pat, and that's terrifying. I'm afraid of letting go and loving someone like that. So many people in my life have let me down. I don't want to get hurt.

But I do want him.

"Am I allowed to coerce you?" Colin inquires.

I chuckle. *"Coerce?"*

"Yeah. Let me show you how good it can be."

He kneels in front of me and proceeds to whip off my leggings and bury his face between my legs.

Fifteen

COLIN

All day, I've been thinking Shay can't possible taste as good as I'm recalling from last night.

I was wrong.

She tastes even better.

I take a moment to inhale her unique feminine scent, and then I'm easing her thong down her slender hips and round ass. We've cleared the air. There's no expectation this can turn into anything more than what it is.

Fuck buddies.

It was crass of me to say it, but Shay brings out the animal in me. I've never hungered for another woman like I've hungered for her. After meeting with Matt, I've counted down the hours until I could come back to her place. Thank God I estimated correctly. I was only waiting for about half an hour before her sultry butt sashayed up the stairs to give me the business about not calling.

Part of me wanted to do as she said and chalk it up to one night, but the other part, the other head, told me no way in hell was I giving up the best sex of my life.

And so here I am in front of her with one of her legs wrapped around my shoulder as I swipe my tongue up her slit. Shay shivers, but I hold her steady, strumming her with my tongue. She moans and tries to squirm away, but now that I've got a hold of her, I'm not letting go. Not until she comes.

My strokes are soft and hard, short and long, until she arches her back off the wall and holds my head to her sex. She's taking her pleasure, and it's a turn-on. She has no idea how much I want her. My dick presses hard against my trousers, and I can't wait to be inside her.

"Don't stop," she begs, arching.

I don't. I want this to be good for her. Adding my fingers to the mix, I wickedly strum her and lose myself in her sweetness. I continue licking, nibbling and laving her until her entire body shudders uncontrollably and she releases a high-pitched scream.

I'm pulling myself into the standing position, but Shay is already reaching for the zip on my trousers. Any doubt about whether we should continue is gone. She's intent on one thing, and that's getting this dick. I aim to please.

She pushes down my pants and briefs and begins stroking me, but I don't want that right now and jerk away. Instead, I draw her to me and claim her lips. I consume her until my lungs beg for air and I have to break the kiss.

She's naked from the waist down and wearing her usual sports bra, but I don't care. I bend her over the side of the couch, taking care to protect us by sliding on a condom, then I'm spreading her legs with one knee and thrusting inside her from behind.

Her inner walls tighten around my shaft. "Fuck!"

I have to take a moment to orient myself. I don't want to come prematurely like some randy teenager.

Slowly, I thrust into her, then harder and harder, pushing her farther into the couch. I have one hand on her hip, the other moves lower until I can pump my fingers in and out her sex, massaging her clit with my thumb.

Shay moans and pushes her ass back to meet my powerful thrusts.

"That's right, baby, just like that." I smack her ass, and she moans even louder. So I do it again, and she lets out a mewl.

A little ass play turns her on? I'll remember that, but right now my focus is burying myself inside Shay's wet heat. We find a fast-paced rhythm that quickly has me losing control. Shay is my match in every way. I lean over her, desperate to take back some of that control, but it's slipping away. I reach in front of her and push her bra upwards so I can pinch her nipple between my thumb and forefinger.

"Yes, Colin, yes." She's getting closer to another orgasm and so am I. My fingers dig into her hips and I pump into her, and when her sex clenches around my dick, I lose the battle.

Later, while sitting at the bar in her kitchen, we end up having the leftovers of the shrimp Florentine Shay made for us the night before. She's wearing my shirt and nothing else, while I've pulled on my boxers.

Our earlier experience was explosive. Is Shay right? Can

we still have a trainer–client relationship with this kind of attraction between us? I don't know. But I also don't want to give up something this good.

Instead, I ask her about her expansion. "Have you put together any numbers?"

She shakes her head. "Nothing formal. Some of us need to actually hire a bookkeeper to make sure it's feasible."

"You don't need to do that." I push the empty plate away on the bar. "You have me. Use me."

"Oh, I'm going to use you," she says with a lascivious smirk.

"I can't wait for that. However, I meant in a professional capacity. Since I'm on medical leave from work, I have nothing but time on my hands. Let me review your financials and come up with a plan."

"Shouldn't you be taking this time to relax and regroup and not take on new work?"

"I need to do something, Shay. Otherwise, I'm going to lose my fucking mind."

"All right. All right." She stands up and goes down another hallway I hadn't paid much attention to before, but I follow her and find it's a second bedroom she's turned into an office/guest room.

She sits at a small desk with her laptop and within seconds, she's printing out several pages. "I assume you want to see my balance sheet and income statement from the last year?"

"That's a start." I accept the papers. "I'll need all your personal expenses along with any checking- or savings-account statements."

She frowns. "I don't know about that."

"I'm not trying to invade your privacy." Uneasiness is written all over her face. "I want to be sure you're not over-extending yourself, but if you want me to focus on Balance and Elevate, that's fine. I'll look these over and come back to you with a plan."

"You would do that?" She sounds surprised.

Have I really been that horrible?

"Yes, of course. You're helping me. It's the least I can do."

"But you're paying me. It doesn't seem like a fair trade."

I start to speak, but she places her fingers over my mouth. "Don't even think about saying what I think you were about to. Our relationship in the bedroom has no place in this conversation."

"Agreed. And I'm doing this because I *want* to. Okay? So let me help."

She releases an audible sigh because she's struggling with accepting my help.

"It'll be fine. I'll review these and get back to you. Sound good?"

She nods. "Okay."

"How about we pick up where we left off?" I plop down on the guest bed.

She pushes me down and comes over to straddle me. "Did you have something in mind?"

"Oh yeah." Unbuttoning my shirt, I push it off her arms, tossing it on the bed. Then I rise so I can latch onto one of her breasts. I suck the nipple into my mouth, and she arches against me, crying out my name. Her small, perfectly sized orbs fit in the palm of my hand and into my mouth like they were made for me.

My fingers cup her flesh, stroking her with long caresses while continuing to suck and nibble. Then I move to the other and give it the same sensuous treatment until Shay rubs against me. I understand. I can't wait to be inside her again, to hear her loud screams. But I don't have a condom with me.

I lift my head, long enough to say, "The condoms are in the other bedroom."

"Are you sure?" To my surprise, she reaches for the shirt on the bed and pulls a condom from the front pocket. The sexy minx came prepared. She slides it on and then eases herself down onto me.

We gasp simultaneously at the intimacy. She leans in, pressing her naked skin against mine, and I tangle my hands in her locs and pull her to me so I can kiss her hard. She kisses me back, winding her arms around my neck, and starts to ride me. Her rhythm is slow, but then our bodies speed up. We're in sync in a way I've not been with other women. I bury my face in her locs and allow my hands to trail down her body until I'm at the place I know will make her quake.

Shay's hold around me tightens, and she lifts herself up and down my dick. Sensations ripple through me, and I grab a handful of her hair, exposing her throat where I suckle her.

"Ah!" I hear the hitch in her voice. She's getting close, but no way am I coming first. I grab hold of her hips and thrust up to meet her. "Colin!"

Her movements become jerky and frantic. I won't last much longer.

Fuck!

"I need you to come, Shay," I urge.

She laughs, and to my surprise the vixen tries to lift off me, but I pull her back down hard. And just like that we both shatter. A kaleidoscope of colors blurs my vision as Shay's muscles contract. She pulls me in and collapses against me. I groan her name as I climax.

This woman has me wrapped around her finger and she doesn't even know it.

I'm in serious trouble.

Sixteen

COLIN

"Let's go hiking," Shay says one Sunday, a few weeks into my training.

"That's a hard pass," I respond, lounging on her sofa.

I don't know how it happened, but I've gotten in the habit of spending my weekends with Shay. When she isn't working at Balance and Elevate, I'm at her place, and we're not just fucking. She's been teaching me how to cook the healthy way with less salt, oil and butter. It's surprisingly tasty once you get used to it, and I'm hoping my cholesterol numbers will be better at the six-week mark when I see the doctor again.

"C'mon." Shay grabs my arm and tries to pull me to my feet. "It's going to be fun. Not only is it great exercise, but you'll enjoy the fresh air and being one with nature."

I laugh at the exuberance in her tone. I've never been the

outdoors type and much prefer the indoor activities we'd been up to earlier. "Wouldn't you rather stay in bed?"

"We did *that* last weekend."

Indeed. She is correct.

Since we started sleeping together, I've learned all the ways to please Shay and vice versa. I know when she wants it hard and fast, or when I need to take my time and draw out the moment. I never imagined I would have this kind of connection with anyone, much less with Shay. This was only supposed to be a fleeting moment, but it's turned into more.

I *like* spending time with her.

"Colin..." Shay folds her arms and pouts. It's so adorable the way her nose crunches up in consternation when she's annoyed with me. How can I say no to her? I don't particularly like walking, let alone hiking. Yet, she's got me walking two miles three times a week as part of my fitness regime.

Sighing, I jump to my feet. "All right, fine. We'll go hiking."

"Yay!" Shay claps her hands in glee. "I'm just going to change." She's wearing one of my T-shirts with nothing else underneath, which made for easy access during this morning's rendezvous. But alas, she's right. We can't stay locked in her apartment forever.

An hour later, we're in Fredericksburg, Texas, and ready to tackle the Enchanted Rock Loop Trail. Turning off the ignition, I exit my Audi and stare at the tree-lined pathways. This is so *not* my speed. It's amazing what we'll do for the people we like.

Shay, however, is pumped. She's opening the trunk and double-checking the backpack she filled before we left. Inside there's refillable water bottles, sandwiches, SunChips, granola bars and dried fruit, a radio, blanket, flashlight and first-aid kit.

"You sure came prepared." I incline my head to the arsenal of goods. "You would think we're getting ready for the zombie apocalypse or something."

Shay shrugs. "You never know. What if we get lost? We need to be ready for the unexpected."

I ignore the idea of getting lost in the woods. "All right, let's do this!" I clap my hands.

I'm trying to psyche myself up that hiking will be fun because at least I'm with a beautiful woman. And Shay is killing it in her running gear. She's got on a wildcat-patterned sports bra and high-waisted bike shorts that hug her ass and have me thinking all kinds of naughty thoughts.

"I'm ready." Shays tries to don the heavy backpack, but I immediately take it from her and swing it over my shoulders.

"Exactly how long is this trail?" I ask, once we're on the move.

"About five point four miles if we do the entire loop," Shay responds, "but we don't have to do all of it. Trust me, I've got you."

And I realize I do. In a short time, Shay has earned my trust and my respect.

I would follow her anywhere.

A few hours later, after we've hiked through grass, dirt roads and trees, we start climbing until eventually we reach a giant rock formation that springs up seemingly out of nowhere.

"Isn't it beautiful?" Shay asks, looking out over the plains. She's not the least bit out of breath, whereas I'm a little winded.

Even though the hike was moderately difficult, we stopped along the way for water breaks. I don't mind the exercise and nature elements because I'm with Shay. She has a way of making me do things I don't like to do.

"Yeah, it is." I come up behind her and wrap my arms around her waist.

She leans back against me, and I inhale her citrusy scent that's now mixed with a fragrance all her own. It makes me want her. This intense attraction will fade. It has to, and before long I'll move on to the future I've planned. But right now, I can't seem to care about any of it. Instead, I spin her around to face me.

She has on sunglasses so I can't see her eyes, but I see her lips. Plush, flagrantly sensual lips that have dragged me over the edge of ecstasy many times. I lower my head and cover her mouth with mine for another taste, and she kisses me back. My hands go to the small of her back, drawing her closer because the kiss is quickly spiking to a fever pitch. But then Shay pulls away.

"We came to hike, Colin," Shay says, somewhat breathlessly.

A grin spreads across my lips. "I know, but..." I glance around, and the entire area is deserted "...we are alone."

"Is that why you came?" she asks. "Because you wanted to change the location where we have sex?"

She sounds disappointed and turns her back to me to start walking back down the hill. Within several long strides, I catch up to her. "Hey, listen, I'm sorry. Today was fun. It wasn't all about sex."

"I just wanted to do something different. Show you something I enjoy," Shay responds.

"And I appreciate that." I want to get back to that easy connection we shared on the way up the trail. "Tell me, when did you start hiking?" I inquire.

"My dad used to take me when he, Riley and I went camping. The elements were too much for Mama so she stayed behind, but I loved the outdoors. Being out in nature was something my father and I shared."

"You don't talk much about your father."

Shay turns to me. "No, I don't. Are you ready for lunch? There's a shady spot down the hill." She points to a patch of trees about a quarter of a mile away. "We can stop there."

I notice she changes the subject from her father quickly, which only makes me curious to know more. Once we've reached our destination, shaken out the blanket, opened the backpack and are tearing into our turkey breast sandwiches with fat-free mayonnaise, I broach the subject again.

"So about your father," I say, taking a bite of my sandwich. "What else did you share a love of besides hiking?"

"Nope. There's nothing more to say about him." She opens her water bottle and takes a long pull.

"You don't have a relationship with him?"

"Why are you pressing the topic?" she snaps. "I don't see you talking about your dad much either."

"You know why. He's gone!" I blurt out. "And I miss him. I would give anything to have him back, to talk to him again or ask his advice."

Shay scoots closer. “I’m sorry, Colin. That was insensitive of me. Of course you miss him. Your relationship with your father sounds much different from mine. Can you tell me about him?”

“We were very close. I looked up to him, you know?” She nods, so I continue. “My dad didn’t come from money. He grew up poor, but he was determined his kids would have a better life. He started out working at a car dealership and was one of their top performers. He was a salesman through and through. He used to tell me there wasn’t anyone he couldn’t upsell. His ambition led to bigger goals like starting his own dealership and, when it became profitable, moving us into an affluent neighborhood. I’ll never forget when he took me into the dealership for the first time and introduced me around. I was so proud of him.

“What an inspiration,” Shay says. “He sounds like a great dad.”

“He was.” I find myself telling more stories, like The Talk when Dad made sure I understood about how not to get a girl pregnant. Or when he helped me buy my first car. All great memories I haven’t thought about in years, let alone shared with another soul. Except with Shay.

“Thank you for bringing me up here, Shay, and pushing me to try new things.”

Her face brightens with a smile, and my heart skips a beat. “You’re welcome.”

There’s something about her that’s comforting yet exciting at the same time. There’s depth to our conversations, more than I’ve ever had in my previous relationships. And that scares me.

Somehow, Shay is not staying in the fuck-buddy category I put her into. Instead, she's becoming something else, something more. Dare I say, a friend.

Seventeen

SHAY

The last month, I've been on a constant high.

The roller-coaster ride goes higher and higher, and even though I'm freaking out a little I don't want it to stop. During the day, I work at the studio, same as usual, teaching yoga and taking care of the business side of it, and some afternoons I train Colin on new moves to strengthen his core and help him relax.

But that's not the only time we're together. We spend weekends shopping for food to ensure Colin stays on his diet. We cook together so he can prepare dishes with less salt and fat to lower his blood pressure and cholesterol. We went hiking the previous weekend because I knew nature would be good for him. He wasn't a fan of the trek, but by the end of the day, even though we were hot and sweaty, Colin thanked me when we reached the summit because I pushed him to do something he'd never done.

The best parts are the nights. I never expected one night with Colin to turn into this smorgasbord of intense passion. We can't seem to assuage the hunger we've developed for each other. He's insatiable for me, and his touch is incredibly addictive. Sometimes, he wakes during the early morning, while I'm still half-asleep, and slides inside me. It's slow and sensual. Most nights, he comes to my place, but tonight, he asked me back to his apartment. He wants to show me the work he's done for my expansion.

His presentation is up on the screen of his large eighty-two-inch television while we sit on a luxurious leather couch. Colin took it upon himself to call the leasing agent for the shopping center and go over rental rates for the suite next door. He has facts and figures on rent costs for the next five years for the studio and the expansion. He's even got preliminary construction numbers and an income projection that has me in the black within the year.

I turn to him. "Are you sure that's right?" I point at the screen in disbelief.

He smiles. "Of course it is. I know my shit."

Laughter bubbles from me. "I'm sorry. I didn't mean to offend you, but how did you put all this together in such a short time?"

"I have my ways." He shrugs. "Besides, you need to get moving before someone else leases that suite." He swipes through the presentation and brings up a document. "I estimated the same rental rate you're paying now with three-percent annual bumps for five years with ten dollars a square foot for tenant improvements, but you'll need to finalize the paperwork with the leasing agent."

"They would give me money to fix the place up?"

Colin nods. "Didn't they do that the last time?"

I shake my head. "No, I took it as-is and did all the work myself."

"Whoever was representing you did you an injustice."

"I represented myself."

"You didn't have an agent?"

"Did I need one?"

"No, but the landlord's agent is always going to look out for their best interest. If you had your own agent, they could have negotiated improvement funds."

My brows furrow in consternation. "How do you know all this stuff?"

"I dabble in commercial real estate from time to time."

"When? In your spare time? I thought you were always working?"

"Up until a year ago, I had more of a life, but then the IPO took over."

"You have to put yourself first again. I challenge you to some self-care, like taking a bath, reading a good book, using a diffuser with calming oils or even getting a massage. There are all kinds of spots you can go to for monthly massages these days."

"Massages, did you say?" Colin's eyes darken and he closes his laptop, placing it on the coffee table. "I know exactly the kind of massage I'd like."

"All in due time. I'm starving. What do you have to eat in here?"

Colin shrugs. "I've eaten most of the meal prep you gave me. How about we go out and grab a bite?"

"Um, sure." I'm surprised because up to now, I'd gotten the distinct impression he didn't want to be seen with me. Other than trips to the grocery store, my studio and the hike we took, we haven't been out in public together. Initially, I was hurt because I felt as if he was embarrassed to be seen with me, but then I looked at it as a positive. When it was over, no one would know and I wouldn't have to explain the demise of this arrangement.

We hop off the couch, and after grabbing my purse, we leave his apartment. As usual, Colin likes to drive his Audi, and we take the elevator to the ground-floor garage where its parked. He's a gentleman and opens my door. Sliding inside, I buckle up. I'm not dressed for anything fancy, but I know just the spot where we can go.

Once he's in the driver's seat, Colin turns to me. "Any thoughts?"

"How about some comfort food?" I give him directions, and fifteen minutes later we're pulling into a parking spot outside Vegan Avenue.

Colin frowns when he turns off the engine. "You picked a vegan restaurant?"

"Why not? Live a little." I open the door and jump out.

Colin stands on the sidewalk looking at the storefront. Reaching for his hand, I tug him toward the door. "C'mon, don't be a chicken. You'll like this. Plus, this is your cheat meal."

A few minutes later, the waitress seats us on the terrace underneath an umbrella. It's a pleasant evening and not too hot.

"I don't know about this Shay..." Colin looks at the menu.

"I promise you'll like it."

"And if I don't?"

"I'll give you that massage."

His eyes light up and he rubs his hands together. "Oh, I'm really *not* going to like it, then."

Colin has no idea what to get so I order for us. When the waitress comes back, I ask for the Avenue Margaritas and nachos to start, a classic vegan burger for Colin and an orange chick'n bowl for me.

"Are you sure about that? It's got quinoa and kale."

"All the veggies you hate," I respond with a smile. "But don't worry, you can taste some of mine."

"You're such a taskmaster," he responds with a smirk.

"You hired me to improve your health, and that's exactly what I'm doing. When's your next doctor's appointment?"

"Monday, the six-week mark. He wants to be sure the medications and my new lifestyle are working."

"He'll be surprised with your lab results because you've stuck to the plan."

His face splits into a grin. "That's because of you."

"You're putting in all the effort and sticking to the meal plan. The reward is you not ending up back in hospital. That's all I want."

"You're very encouraging, Shay."

The waitress returns with our margaritas, and after taking a long luxurious sip, I lean back in my chair. "Did you just give me a compliment?"

"Yeah, don't let it go to your head." There's a glint of humor in his eyes, and it tells me he's sincere. That means a lot. I take pride in what I do, and getting him healthy is my top priority.

And healthy can be delicious. Evidenced by the nachos—with crunchy tortilla chips, black beans, pico de gallo, guacamole and soyrizo, covered with cashew queso and sprinkled with jalapeños.

"Is there meat on that?" Colin asks.

"Well, it's soyrizo, sort of like chorizo. Try it!"

He shakes his head, so I lift a nacho piled with fixings and push it toward his mouth. Colin eyes me warily before opening his mouth and accepting the nacho. His eyes grow wide as he chews. "This is pretty good."

I'm vindicated. "Told ya."

Colin is lifting a nacho to my lips when a woman's voice says, "Colin, is that you?"

He quickly lowers his hand, and his face changes from teasing and flirtatious to wearing an expression of guilt. A beautiful, statuesque woman with skin the color of ginger and flowing honey-brown hair that wafts past her shoulders comes to stand by our table. She's wearing jeans, a silky black top and a white blazer. She's very put-together for a place like this and *so* not like me. Her face, however, is oddly familiar.

Colin rises to his feet. "Claire, it's good to see you. Do you remember Shay Davis? We went to high school together."

One of her heavily arched eyebrows rise. "Oh my God! Shay Davis. Weren't you and your friends called the Sextuplets or something?"

My ire rises. "No, Claire. We're the Six Gems. You remember Egypt? She's the one who wanted to kick your ass." I'm not about to let this heifer throw shade at me or my girls.

Claire is about to come back with a smart remark when

Colin intervenes. "Now, now. That was over a decade ago. Surely we've moved on, haven't we?" He glares at me as if I'm in the wrong.

My arms fold across my chest, and I dare the bitch to say something else about my friends who will be here in San Antonio next weekend for Wynter's wedding. The look on my face must tell Claire I'd cut a bitch, because she retreats and plasters on a fake-ass smile.

"Of course, Colin. That's all in the past. I'm just surprised to see you here…" Her words linger and there's no mistaking she meant to finish *with her.*

Colin pulls Claire to the side, and I can't hear what he says because he's standing with his back to me, shielding them from me. Whatever. I continue eating the nachos, but now they taste sour. The entire evening does.

When did Colin reconnect with Claire? When has he had time? He never mentioned it, but why should he? We're just fuck buddies, right?

Their conversation ends, and Claire makes sure to say loud enough for me to hear, "I can't wait to see you again." Of course he would date her, because she's the kind of girl Colin wants. She comes from a high-class, prominent family in the community with an Ivy League education to boot. I come from a broken, middle-class household and never went to college. We couldn't be more different.

He comes back to our table. "Sorry about that. I had no idea we would run into Claire."

"She acted as if you guys are close. We didn't discuss exclusivity, but what the hell, Colin? Are you seeing her? Are you sleeping with both of us? Call me old-fashioned, but I only sleep with one man at a time."

He shakes his head furiously. "No, of course not. I'm not a player, Shay. Never have been. When I'm with a woman, she's the only one I focus on. I'm with you right now and not with her."

"Meaning?" He needs to be clear about what he's saying, because I'm starting to feel some kind of way.

"I'm not sleeping with her."

"But you want to?" I complete his thought. "I can see it in your eyes. You still want her."

"Listen, Shay." And those two words cut like a knife. "You're amazing. Smart, ambitious and sexy, and you sure as hell like to challenge me, but I'm not going to lie. Claire is the type of woman I'm used to dating."

My nose scrunches in distaste. "And what am I? Chopped liver?"

"Of course not, that came out all wrong."

Rising to my feet, I snatch my purse off the back of the chair. "Oh no, it came out exactly right. Claire is the kind of woman you want to marry, but I'm just the one you like to fuck. If you want to be with a high-society woman from an affluent background, then do it. I won't stand by and be mistreated by any man."

That's what my mom did. She knew my father was cheating, but it was okay so long as he stayed with her. When he left her for his mistress, Mama fell apart.

Pushing past him, I head for the door. I don't need this kind of hassle in my life. It's why I don't do relationships of any kind: because I don't want to get hurt. And seeing how Colin looked at Claire was like a dagger to my heart. Who gives a fuck about dinner? The night is over, and I want to go home. Once on the sidewalk, I pull out my phone and call an Uber.

Damn it. The closest one is eleven minutes out.

I pace the sidewalk.

This isn't a tourist area with a bunch of rideshares and taxis around. I'll have to wait, which means I might see him.

Several minutes later, there's a presence beside me. Colin is holding a bag. "It's our dinner." He lifts it up.

I roll my eyes and face the street.

"Shay." When I continue to ignore him, Colin grabs my arm. "I'm sorry for what I said back there. It was callous and hurtful."

I give him a side-eye. "Yes, it was." Anger courses through me, so much so it feels as if I can spit nails.

"I like you, Shay. And is there history with Claire? Yes. But I'm not with her right now. I'm with you. Because I want to be. Please get in the car and let me take you back home."

"There's no need. I called an Uber."

"Cancel it!"

My expression hardens when I face him. "Don't order me around, Colin."

"I'm not trying to. I'm sorry. I put my foot in my mouth back there, and I'm doing my best to apologize, but you have to let me. I'm sorry, okay? I didn't mean to make you feel less-than because you don't come from a well-to-do family like me or Claire. You're an amazing woman who I happen to like a lot. I enjoy spending time with you. We were having a good night before Claire came. Let's not end on a bad note. *Please* cancel the Uber."

His pleading tone gives me pause, and I glance up. His expression is one of remorse, and I'm not one to hang on to anger, except maybe when it comes to my father. "Fine." Snatching the bag, I swiftly walk to the passenger door of his Audi. He opens the door, and once inside I cancel the Uber.

He joins me on the driver's side. "Thank you."

"You're welcome. And to make it up to me, you can give me a massage. You owe me."

A slow smile spreads across his face. "With pleasure."

An hour later, the pleasure is all mine because Colin has me naked on my bed while he pours massage oils into his palms. I hear smacking sounds and then his warm palms are on my back. He kneads and massages my shoulders and back, relaxing the tension after our exchange about Claire. Then he moves lower, to my ass, where he strokes my cheeks up and down until my sex tightens with wanting him inside me.

Instead of Colin's dick, I get his tongue at my lower lips. He uses his fingers to spread me wide so he can feast on my slickened flesh with an intensity I didn't know was possible. He strums my clit with light flicks of his tongue while his finger slips inside me, coaxing moans from my body.

"Oh my God!" The sheets bunch within my viselike grip as he laps me with his tongue so furiously my orgasm is explosive.

I lie shivering on the bed, and Colin leans down. "Am I forgiven?"

"Yes."

For a little while I forget he wants a bitch like Claire instead of me.

Claire is desirable because she has the status, wealth and background that I don't or won't ever have. I'm not good enough for him, just like I wasn't a good enough wife for Kevin because I couldn't carry our babies. Just like I wasn't a good enough daughter to make my dad stay. Will some-one, Colin included, ever see my value? And now that our fuck-buddy relationship has suddenly become more com-plicated, will he renege so can spend time with Claire? Do I need to worry about Balance and Elevate's future?

Eighteen

COLIN

"I'm surprised at how well you're doing, Colin," Dr. Nelson tells me at my six-week check-up.

"That's a good thing, right?"

I've been working with Shay this entire time, and she's pushed me to do things outside my comfort zone. We do yoga most days, but she's incorporated Pilates into our workouts not only to keep it interesting but also to challenge me. And the morning walks, after our enthusiastic nights in bed, are keeping me fit.

"Of course. I'm thrilled. Your HDL and LDL numbers are lower. Even your A1C has improved. But the last time you were here you were pretty hesitant about my advice."

"You're right, doc. I was, but after I thought about it, I knew I had to make a change."

"What have you done differently? What's the secret sauce?"

"I hired a fitness instructor. She owns her own yoga studio and is a licensed nutritionist."

"That's excellent. A very smart move."

"She has an alternative way of exercising that honestly I would never have attempted on my own, but I ran into her after my angina attack, and I guess it was fate or something."

"Whatever you're doing with her, keep it up," Dr. Nelson replies. "Your numbers still aren't in the normal range, but the lab results speak for themselves. You're on the right track."

"Thank you. When I make up my mind to do something, I do it."

"I'd like to see you back here in another six weeks and we'll reevaluate where you are then. Sound good?"

"Sounds good, doc."

After I make my follow-up appointment and walk to my car, I immediately call Shay. She picks up on the second ring. "Guess what?"

"Your numbers are lower?"

I feel like a balloon that's been deflated. "How did you know?"

She lets out a peal of laughter from the other end of the line. "It's what I do, Colin. Help people improve their nutrition and overall health."

"I have to tell you, you're worth every penny I'm paying you."

"Damn right I am," she responds. "I told you with the right diet and exercise you would see improvement."

"You're good at what you do, Shay, and I apologize for ever doubting you."

"Thank you and you're welcome. I've got to go. I have another class. We'll talk later."

After ending the call, I'm at a loss. I don't have a session with Shay, but I'm so excited by my doctor's visit I want to celebrate. But celebrating personal news is not the type of relationship Shay and I have. It's about sex. A lot of sex.

Shay and I have had sex everywhere in her apartment. Up against the wall. The kitchen counter. The couch. Her bed. The shower. The floor.

My mind incessantly thinks about ways to please her, and she has an appetite as insatiable as mine. There's never been another woman so compatible with me in the bedroom. Or out of it, my inner voice says. At first, we were enemies, but we've moved beyond that. I consider Shay a friend.

My wild, hot sexy friend who I like to fuck.

But we talk too. She has a wicked sense of humor and doesn't mind the nerdy side of me, like watching *Marvel* movies or playing *Fortnite*. I doubt Claire would even consider the possibility of sharing those experiences with me.

Even though I ran into her at Thea's and at the vegan restaurant, I still haven't called her for a date. First off, it wouldn't be fair to Shay. I'm no liar. I'm a one-woman kind of man, and I don't intend on starting something with Claire when I'm not done with Shay yet. We're working whatever *this* is out of my system while I'm getting healthy. Only then can I move forward in the way my father always wanted me to, build my success and start my life with Claire.

Sometimes, I wish Shay was that woman. A sophisticated socialite from a connected, affluent family who could be my plus-one at company parties. It would be so much easier if I could roll them into one woman.

But then, Shay wouldn't be who she is—the vibrant, sexy, caring woman I can't stop fantasizing about.

My mother is my next call, and I arrange to take her out for dinner. It's been too long since we spent quality mother–son time together. She is surprised but thrilled at the invite. So here I am, pulling into the driveway of my childhood home. She's already outside waiting for me.

Sometimes I wonder how she's able to live in the house that holds so many memories of Dad. I'm not sure I could. The memories would suffocate me. As it is, it's hard to be home because I'm waiting for Dad to walk in the door to tell us about his day at the dealership or give me a piece of advice about school or my career. Or just lend a listening ear.

I miss him.

Losing him was like losing my best friend. I suppose that's why I feel the loss every day. I never want to go through that kind of loss again. Instead, I work on achieving the goals we set before he passed away. He was the one who told me when I found the right woman, a woman like Claire, I should hold on to her. I couldn't do it back then, but I'm hoping I can do it now.

"Hey, Ma." I open the car door for her.

"Honey, I'm so happy you called me," she says, sliding into the passenger seat. "It was such a pleasant surprise."

"We should do it more often," I respond once we're buckled in. "I'm sorry I don't come around as much I should."

"Oh, I get it," my mother says. "Your father was such a

larger-than-life personality, there's a void here without him. You think I don't know that?"

"I know you do. You more than anyone. You were married for twenty-seven years."

"Twenty-seven wonderful years." While on the drive, mom talks about her life with my father, and I find myself enthralled listening to their love story. It's not like I haven't heard it all before, but I guess this time it's different.

"Is everything all right?" she asks, once we're seated at her favorite seafood restaurant.

"Everything's fine. Why do you ask?" I look up from the menu I was studying.

"You've got something on your mind. Or you're conflicted about something. Or maybe someone?"

How is it that mothers can pick up on what you're not saying? "There is someone."

She snaps her fingers. "I knew it. Is it Claire? Are you dating again?"

My smile wanes. "It's not Claire."

My parents loved Claire. She had a way of wrapping them around her pinkie finger. They would leave us, seventeen-year-old teenagers, alone in the house, showing me how much they trusted us even then. My father always told me Claire was a keeper.

But it's not so simple now. The more I get to know Shay and see the sides of her she doesn't reveal to anyone else, the more I like her. It's not going to be easy to pick up where I left off with Claire, as if Shay never existed. Just the thought makes me uneasy.

Her mouth forms an *O.* "Who is it, then? Is it someone I know?"

"I don't think so."

"Is there a problem?"

I nod. "Yeah, she's nothing like the women I usually date. She's not a woman you would expect to see me with."

My mother frowns. "Why would there be an expectation? You like who you like."

"I'm usually with someone more polished and elegant."

"And this other woman, she's neither of those things?"

"No, but she's down-to-earth. You know, real. She doesn't dress up or put on airs. She is who she is."

"I like her already." When I frown, my mother asks, "Is that a problem?"

"I like her too much, and I didn't think I would. Quite frankly, I thought I had it all figured out. I'd date Claire, we'd marry, and that would be the end of it. Dad liked her."

"But this new woman has thrown a monkey wrench into your carefully laid plans?"

I nod begrudgingly.

"Colin," my mother says and reaches across the table and grabs my hand, "you've always tried to plan everything in your life. You've been this way since you were a little boy. When everyone was outside playing, you'd be deciding on what you would wear to school the next day or doing your schoolwork ahead of time. *Listen,* I know you loved your father, but he wasn't without his flaws, and it sounds like he was looking at the superficial. This is your life. Your future. Sometimes you have to go with your gut. Who feels right to you?"

"My gut?"

"Yeah, what's it telling you? If it's telling you this woman, whose name you've yet to share..."

A deep chuckle escapes my lips. "I'm sorry, Mom. It's Shay. Shay Davis."

"Sometimes you can't plan who you're going to fall for, my boy. And if Shay is who you want, you can't be afraid to go after her because she doesn't fit in this perfect box you've designed for your life."

"Aw, Mom, I'm not saying that. I'm just confused is all."

"If you say so, Colin."

After lunch and I drop her off, I think about what she said. Who do I really want? I've always followed the directives my father gave me because I respected him and wanted the kind of love story he and Mom had. But maybe mine is different. I don't have to take my father's advice. Not if it means following plans that don't seem to fit anymore. I need to start following my own path, what's right for me. Which leads me to wonder...

Am I falling for Shay?

It certainly wasn't something I wanted or even planned, but now that the thought is in my head, it takes residence there. How does Shay feel about me? Would she be open to exploring this relationship beyond the physical?

I'm afraid to ask her.

Because I'm afraid she might just say *yes.*

Nineteen

SHAY

My relationship with Colin over the last week hasn't gone back to the way it was pre-Claire. We work out together three times a week, but we haven't made plans to meet up afterward like we did previously. I thought Colin wanted me for sex, but even that feels like it's off the table because he has Claire waiting in the wings.

He said she's the type of woman he'd like to be with long-term, and the knowledge makes me feel how I felt with Kevin: not good enough. After the miscarriages, I felt less-than because I couldn't fulfill what I thought was my purpose, having a family of my own. Since the divorce, I've let ambition fuel me, let my career be the focus. What choice did I have?

And now, I don't have a choice with Colin either.

We're not a couple. We're just friends with benefits. Fuck buddies. It's my fault. I agreed to a sexual relationship only.

If I want to change things, I have to tell Colin I want more. I'm not interested in a sex-only situation anymore.

We blurred the lines. We called each other, had dinners together, cuddled. I'm starting to trust Colin, when in the past trust has been difficult. My father's abandonment and the divorce hurt me, so it's hard for me to be vulnerable. I hate this feeling of uncertainty.

I don't know what Colin wants from me.

On cue, I do what I do best and push aside my feelings and move forward with Balance and Elevate. This afternoon, I'm meeting a commercial real estate agent. He's arranged an official tour of the store next door, and we're going to talk about my expansion goals.

When I arrive at the bakery, a dark-haired gentleman with baby blue eyes is already there, dressed in a suit with a white speckled tie. I'm glad I decided on a black-and-cream color-block sheath dress with a side slit and high-heeled sandals. I don't own many dresses, but there are a few in my arsenal.

"Mr. Hoffman?"

"You must be Shay." Darryl offers a warm smile.

"Yes, I am. Thank you for setting up this meeting."

"Of course. When Colin mentioned you needed representation, it was a no-brainer. I rep all sorts of clients, so it'll be my pleasure to help you." He opens the door of the storefront, and the chime goes off.

Mr. Yang greets us and rushes over to shake my hand. "Shay, I'm so glad you will be able to take over. The store is just too much for me with my wife in poor health."

"I'm sorry, Mr. Yang. But it's you who is doing me a service."

"Allow me to show you around," Mr. Yang replies. He gives us a tour of the entire bakery from front to back.

"What do you think?" Darryl asks afterward.

"It's perfect, but it's going to need a lot of work. Colin mentioned you might be able to negotiate with the landlord on some funds for improving the space?"

"Oh, absolutely," Darryl replies. "Since you sent me your lease a couple days ago, I was able to review it. You still have two years left on your term. If you're interested in extending another four years, it might persuade the landlord. You would have a five-year deal on the expansion and an additional three years on your existing space, both suite leases would be co-terminus."

I nod approvingly. "Yes, I would like that. The studio is doing great, and my forecast shows that continuing."

"Excellent! I'll contact the landlord and ask for a proposal, and we'll go from there." He offers his hand.

"Thank you for all your help, Mr. Hoffman. I look forward to receiving the proposal." I enthusiastically shake his hand. We're leaving the shop when Colin's Audi pulls into the parking lot.

When Darryl sees Colin, he waits, and the two men exchange pleasantries before Colin walks toward me.

"Darryl tells me everything went well?" Colin asks.

"It did, but you didn't have to come today," I respond, unlocking the studio door. Colin follows me inside. We're not open for business yet so I lock the door behind me. "We don't have a class, do we?"

A frown mars his attractive features. "No, but I wanted to check on the meeting, make sure Darryl took good care of you."

Is that concern in his voice? I don't get it. Colin made it clear he's not interested in dating me or being with me long-term. I'm not his kind of woman when it comes to relationships, yet, he invites himself to my business meeting?

"The showing went well. Darryl will send me a proposal."

Colin claps his hands. "That's excellent."

"Was there something else?" I want a boundary between us, but that's hard to maintain if he steps over it. His emotional support will make me want more from him than he's willing to give.

His normally smooth brow furrows more deeply, and the lines around his mouth etch tightly. "Actually, yes, you look beautiful today. But different."

My eyes narrow. "You sound surprised that I can be professional, Colin. Is it really that shocking I can put on a nice dress from time to time?" Annoyed, I push past him and head to my office.

"I'm not surprised," he says from my doorway. "Can't I acknowledge you're a beautiful woman?"

Well, that shuts me down. He's made me feel beautiful, but he's never called me that before. "Of course you can. Thank you."

"You don't have to thank me, Shay." He eats up the space between us and pulls me into his arms. "I've always thought so. Can't you tell? I can't get enough of you."

Not this week.

It's because he doesn't think I'm good enough to brush

shoulders with his corporate folks. I may not come from money, I may not have graduated from an Ivy League school, but I know how to treat people.

And he's been decidedly cool toward me since we ran into Claire, and now he thinks I'm beautiful? I don't know what to make of Colin sometimes. He's hot and cold. Either way, I refuse to let myself be defined by his desires. I won't be like Mom and allow my mood and life to revolve around a man. I will focus on B&E.

Using my palms, I push against Colin's hard chest until he releases me.

"What's wrong?"

"You tell me. The last week, you've been busy." I hate the sound of desperation in my voice.

"I thought you would appreciate a little time to yourself," Colin says. "I've been monopolizing your time."

"You have."

"Then, why does it sound like you're mad at me?" Colin says. "Please don't me mad. Come back to my apartment after class. I want to make you the brussels sprouts recipe I found."

I *am* mad at Colin, but I refuse to let him know how much his actions over the last week have hurt. "All right, I'll come over to your place."

I don't want him to realize I've caught *feelings*, so unexpected after all this time. Once, I imagined never feeling this way again. I was dead inside, but somehow Colin brought me back to life.

Later, after Colin makes me filet mignon and brussels sprouts for dinner, we lay curled up on his couch watching one of his *Marvel* movies. I've changed out of the sheath dress and into my usual yoga attire. Earlier, it felt awkward and stilted between us, but when I arrived at his place, he lifted my face to his and kissed me hard.

Maybe he did miss me after all?

I ignore the misgivings about whether Colin thinks I'm good enough because, if I'm honest, I've missed being in his arms. I don't want to feel this way. I don't want to miss him, to want more from him than he can give. Why can't I have sex and not care? Guess it's not in my DNA.

My cell phone rings. I swipe right, and the Six Gems are on the call. "Hey, girls."

"Hello to you too, Shay," Teagan says with lots of attitude.

"Um, why am I getting shade from you?"

"Did you forget you were supposed to pick me up from the airport?" Lyric asks.

Shit! Shit! Shit! I forgot the Gems were coming in tonight for Wynter's wedding this weekend. I've been so caught up in Colin and his mixed messages that I lost sight of my friends. It's so unlike me. Usually I'm all about my girls and making sure we are there for each other. This just proves I'm getting in too deep with Colin. I need to pull back.

"Luckily, we ran into Egypt and Garrett at the airport, and they were kind enough to let us tag along with them," Lyric states.

"I'm so sorry. Where are you now?"

Teagan rolls her eyes. "We are at our hotel, missy. Where the hell are you?" She peers into the screen. "That's not your place. Who are you with?"

Suddenly, Colin is beside me and mouthing who is that? I shake my head, but he's not taking the hint. Instead, he grabs my leg and pulls me down until I'm flat on my back on the sofa.

"No one," I lie, trying to hold the phone up so the Gems can't see him.

Colin doesn't like that answer, and his eyes narrow. Within seconds, he's pulling off my yoga pants and snatching down my thong until my lower half is completely bare. A wicked smirk crosses his face. Then he leans between my thighs and tastes me.

I want to howl and scream, but I have an audience.

"I don't believe that for a second," Egypt responds. "You do realize we have to get Wynter to the finish line in a couple of days?"

"Yes, but Wynter knows I'm here, and if she needs my help all she has to do is call."

Colin swirls his tongue and presses it against my clit. If I react, the girls will know something is up.

"Well, then pull your shit together and get ready to be a bridesmaid," Teagan says, "because the squad is here."

Colin licks, sucks and nibbles on my clit, pushing me to the edge, but then he stops long enough for me to manage "Y-yes, I will," even though he is doing wicked things to me with his mouth.

"And tell whoever it is that you're fucking," Asia adds, "we plan on meeting him while we're here."

And with that, the Gems blessedly end the call and Colin dives back in with gusto. "Colin," I pant and drop the phone to the floor. Air barely fills my lungs because the man sinks two fingers inside me, twisting them while his thumb and tongue brush against my clit.

"Why didn't you tell me Wynter's wedding is this weekend?" he asks, looking up at me.

"I—I..." I can't think when he's got me on the edge.

His hands and mouth stop as he waits for my answer.

"Don't stop. I'm so close."

His eyes narrow. "Then, answer me."

"In case you don't remember, I've been a little busy with you. But the Gems are right. I need to focus on Wynter for the next couple of days. And for your information, the wedding is on Saturday."

Colin eyes me suspiciously and then greedily feasts on me again. My breathless moans float into the air, and I writhe from his skillful tongue. My body belongs to him, and he knows it. He pulls back again. "And the wedding?"

"Um, what about it?" I growl, desperate for him to finish what he started.

"Are you going solo?" He dips his head to lick and twirl his tongue with masterful strokes, and I roll my hips, letting his fingers and tongue do their work.

"Y-yes, w-why?"

"What do you think?" He withdraws his fingers and tongue and I lift up from the sofa, resting on my forearms. He's pushing his sweatpants and boxers over his hips and down his legs.

"You want to come with me to the wedding?"

"Don't sound so enthusiastic," Colin responds, stroking a condom over his very impressive erection.

My first reaction is to say something snarky back, but I

lick my lips at the thought of having him inside me again. He moves between my parted legs. Gripping my ankles, he positions them over his shoulders and plunges inside. Deep, but somehow not deep enough.

"Colin, I need more," I beg.

"And the wedding?" he inquires, slowly withdrawing.

I will say anything right now to get him to fuck me. I need his dick. "Yes, if you want to come, you're invited."

"Oh, I'm going to come." He thrusts so hard into me that he fills me completely.

I want to cry out, yes, but I don't want to give him the satisfaction. I just want him to take me. And he does. Using one hand, he grips my hips and drives into me relentlessly while the other squeezes and fondles my already tight breasts. My vision clouds as he stamps my body with his. He keeps up a steady rhythm, and I close my eyes.

"Open your eyes."

Startled, my lids lift, and the emotions in his dark gaze are raw and needy. I love this side to Colin, when he's unguarded and being one-hundred-percent real with me. He continues a frantic pace, slamming into me and bringing me closer to the oblivion I seek. There's nothing for me to hold onto so I eventually surrender.

My scream sounds around the room. Colin's body goes rigid, and he curses. "Fuck!" He drives into me one last time.

Like always, it's perfect, and I realize I'm totally dick-whipped.

Twenty

COLIN

Staring into my closet, there's nothing but a row of suits. Any number of them will work for an afternoon-to-evening wedding, but the question is, why am I going?

Why was I so insistent that Shay include me?

Could it be because she hadn't told her friends about me?

Am I her dark secret?

Isn't she yours?

Quite possibly.

Yet last night, I was hurt Shay didn't want to acknowledge me or our relationship by mentioning me on the phone, or inviting me to the wedding on her own. She must have felt the same way—insignificant? unimportant? —the evening we saw Claire and I didn't claim any sort of relationship with her. I don't like feeling this way, and I'm guessing Shay didn't either.

A relationship with Shay was never meant to be serious.

I was supposed to exorcise her from my system with some great sex. Instead, I discovered a genuine, kind and giving woman who cares about her family and friends. A great teacher. A fantastic conversationalist. An ambitious businesswoman. And a passionate lover.

A woman so different from Claire Watson.

I've had Claire's number for a while and still haven't used it. I once thought she was my ideal woman. I should be jumping at the chance to go out with her. But something is holding me back. I tell myself it's because I'm fixing my health issues. Because I don't want to start a relationship in my current condition. Because there's still work, and I don't know where I stand at the company.

But deep down, I know it's Shay.

And now I have an invite to this wedding. By attending, Shay's friends may think we're more when we've just been kickin' it. But it's not like I can take it back. I was the one who didn't play fair to get her to agree to invite me.

Jesus, I'm a mess.

I'm glad she's busy today doing girlie stuff with the Gems and enjoying the rehearsal dinner later tonight. It gives me time to think about something else, like spending time with my sister and niece. The time off has allowed me to develop a bond with Kira. She's growing so fast I don't want to miss another moment.

After deciding which suit I'll wear tomorrow, I head out of my apartment. Twenty minutes later, I pull into Thea's driveway. I ring the doorbell, but no one answers. That's when I hear laughter coming from the back of the house.

I descend the stairs and walk to the rear. Thea is outside with Kira, tossing my niece up in the air.

"Hey, sis."

Thea jumps when she hears my voice and clutches Kira on her chest.

My hands fly up. "Sorry, didn't mean to startle you."

"What are you doing here?" Thea asks, placing Kira in the large playpen. There's lots of toys inside, which quickly garner her attention, leaving us time to talk.

"How's it going with the personal trainer and health coach you told me about?" Thea inquires, after we sit across from Kira on matching lawn chairs.

"Great. She's helped me make better decisions with my nutrition and reduce my stress. My doctor saw improvement in my numbers. When I first started training with her, I wasn't one-hundred-percent certain her new-age methods would work, but I'm more relaxed, sleeping a solid seven to eight hours a night, which has never happened before. I'm actually doing yoga, if you can believe it."

"Get the fuck out of here." Thea laughs.

She's shocked by the change in me because it's so far out of my comfort zone, but Shay has made the experience of changing easier. And it has nothing to do with our personal relationship. She's a good instructor. She's patient, kind and willing to help when I can't do some of the more involved movements.

"It's crazy, Thea. Believe me. But I had to do something drastic to change my life, and yoga has been a good bet. I might even try meditation."

She laughs. "I can't see you doing meditation."

"I'm open to it. Shay wants me to give it a try."

"Who's Shay?"

"My trainer." Thea nods, and I wonder what she's thinking. "What's up?"

She shrugs. "I don't know. You seem happier. Does Shay have something to do with that?"

My face scrunches into a frown. "I do?"

"Yeah, you do, and I'm glad. After Dad died, it seemed like you felt you had to step up and be the man of the house. Maybe between grief and the job, it was too much responsibility."

"It was a lot to handle," I respond, "but I did it because it's what Dad would have wanted. The problem is I was so busy helping other people and my company, I didn't take care of myself, but I am now, thanks to Shay."

Labeling us fuck buddies was a misnomer. She will always be more than that. Shay has been a positive influence in all areas of my life. Spending more time with my family is a bonus, and that too is what my father would have wanted.

Kira finds one of her noise-making toys and starts banging it against the playpen.

"I think that's our cue," I say, but instead of letting Thea get up, I do. I lift the five-month-old baby in my arms. Kira smiles at me. She recognizes me. Since I've been on medical leave, I've made it a point to stop by often, and it's made a difference in our relationship.

Kira has put on some weight. She's not the newborn I held in the palm of my hand when she was first born. I was afraid to break her or not hold her head right, but now my niece is alert and very active.

I'm sad Dad isn't here to meet his granddaughter. Out of nowhere, my eyes well with tears, and my heart rate speeds up. He was taken away from us much too soon. It's why I'm trying to do better and be there for my family, but it's hard trying to live up to his expectations for every aspect of my life. Especially when his idea of success goes against what I want.

"Where did you meet Shay?" Thea resumes her line of questioning once I'm holding Kira.

I was hoping she would forget, and we could move on to another topic of conversation. "At a smoothie shop," I respond, "but it goes back further than that. We went to high school together."

"Really? Like you and Claire? Did you guys all know each other? Speaking of Claire, how's that going?"

Damn. Another question I don't want to answer, but I reply honestly. "Yes, we all knew each other back in the day, but Shay and Claire were never friends. They had their own crowds. As for Claire and me…" I sigh "… I haven't pulled the trigger on that."

"What?" Thea cries. "I thought she was the one who got away? Or at least that's what you've always said. I thought you'd be jumping at the chance to get back with her."

"She was—I mean she *is* the one, but I'm not in a good place, Thea. I nearly had a heart attack. I'm on medical leave from my job. I need to have my shit together before I approach a woman like Claire."

"Is that the only reason?"

"What else would there be?" I ignore the thought of Shay that enters my mind by bouncing Kira up and down on my knee to her utter amusement. She laughs and giggles.

"In the meantime, you'll hang out with Shay?"

I turn to look at her. "What do you mean?"

"C'mon, Colin. I'm not blind. Something is up with you and your trainer."

"There's nothing going on. We're friends." I don't want Thea to comment on my friends-with-benefits situation with Shay so I keep the party line.

"Stop fooling yourself. You've got it bad for Shay, and the sooner you own up to it, the better."

If my mother and sister can see it, then these feelings for Shay are obvious, undeniable. Yet I'm conflicted.

Aren't I supposed to want Claire? But Shay is beautiful too—sexy and compassionate and ambitious.

It doesn't matter to me that she doesn't come from a moneyed background or wear high-end clothes or have a degree from a fancy college—even though a small part of me thinks it *should* matter. The part that still can't let go of my plans for success.

Shay and I connect on so many levels.

I'm not sure if I can give her up, or if I even want to.

I don't want to.

At least not yet.

Shay and I are not over.

Twenty-One

SHAY

"All right, chick, we want all the details," Asia says when I make it to the day spa Wynter rented out for the entire bridal party, including her mother.

When I arrived, the Gems were already in the locker room, undressing and putting on the plush pink robes with our names printed on the front. Each of our titles, such as *Maid of Honor* or *Bridesmaid*, is engraved on the back. I wanted to slide in without being noticed, but Egypt puts me on blast as soon as I walk in.

She steps in front of me. "And where do you think you're going? You owe us an explanation for last night."

"I second that emotion." Lyric snaps her fingers. Her long auburn hair is already in a neat ponytail and sways when she speaks.

"All right, I'll tell you," I respond, "but where is the bride?"

"I'm right here!" Wynter yells from behind us. She's wearing a white robe that says *Bride.*

I rush toward Wynter and envelop her in a huge hug. "Congratulations! I'm so happy for you."

"I can't believe the wedding is tomorrow. I've been planning and waiting for over a year," Wynter replies.

"You're the one who let your mama take over and create a big society wedding," Teagan states.

Wynter shrugs. "I did. She wanted it so badly. I didn't have the heart to refuse her."

"After the way she behaved in the past…you're a better woman than me."

"I'm the woman I am," Wynter says, glancing around the room, "because of each of you. You held me up during life's difficult times and supported me during my happiest times. So thank you."

"You're making me emotional." Lyric wipes a tear from her cheek.

"Me too." Asia sniffs into a Kleenex. "But that's because I have too many hormones running through me during my second trimester, so forgive me."

We all laugh, and that's how the afternoon starts—with talking and laughter. Once we're all seated at our respective pedicure stations, the questions about my disappearing act resurface.

"So, Shay…" The bride is the one stirring the pot this time. "Why don't you share with us why you weren't able to pick up the Gems?"

Of course they would put Wynter up to do the asking. I

can't refuse her when this day is all about her. "I was otherwise engaged."

"With who?" Egypt presses. "A girl has to have details."

"I was with a client."

"That late?" Asia snorts. "Shay, I'm calling bullshit before you even attempt to finish that lie. If I were a betting woman, I would say you were getting busy, which is why you left us hanging at the airport."

"Boom!" Teagan fakes like she's dropping a mic.

I roll my eyes. No way are they letting me off the hot seat.

"You've been caught, girlfriend." Asia points at me. "Just fess up."

"Inquiring minds would like to know," Egypt says from the opposite chair.

"You guys are terrible! Okay, okay, I'm guilty as charged," I yell.

"Whew!" Lyric wipes fake sweat off her brow. "Why we got to twenty-question you? Who cares if you were getting busy?" She rolls her hips in the pedicure chair in a sexual motion.

My face flushes with embarrassment. "I'll bring him tomorrow, and you can interrogate him yourself."

"We have to wait? No way!" Asia shakes her head. "You can't keep me in suspense. It's not good for a pregnant lady."

"Oh, don't go pulling that card, missy." I wag my finger. "Our focus is on Wynter and not my sex life. Wouldn't you agree?" I turn to the bride-to-be.

Wynter nods in agreement. "Of course."

I escape the Gems' inquisition for now, but I'm on borrowed time. Tomorrow, my friends will want to know about my relationship with Colin. They'll expect me to discuss what it means—is it casual or something more? The Gems will push me to face my fears and express my true feelings for Colin.

What do I tell them when I don't completely understand them myself?

After the pedicures and manicures, the ladies return to their hotel and I drive to my apartment to change for the rehearsal dinner later that evening.

I love when the Gems get together. Our camaraderie and sisterhood have an ease I've never found with other people. Usually, I tell them anything, but today, I held back. I was afraid to tell them about me and Colin.

They won't judge me, but maybe I'm judging myself for jumping so easily into a sexual relationship when there is no chance for a future? I don't usually fall into bed with men I hardly know, but Colin has been different from the start. Even when we were frenemies, there was an undeniable spark between us.

And now that we've become lovers, it's so much more. My mouth twists. Here I go again fantasizing about the way Colin looks me at when he's inside me…the way he touches me so reverently…the way he makes love to me…

Stop.

When it comes to our fuck-buddy situation, I can't have my head in the clouds. It's just mind-blowing, toe-curling, headboard-banging sex. Colin hasn't caught *feelings.* He's not looking for a long-term relationship with someone like me. I'm good enough to satiate his lust, but not good enough to mingle with his corporate colleagues.

It makes me think back to my marriage, how I felt incomplete. Not good enough to be a mother because I couldn't carry my babies to term. Kevin even threw it in my face that I focused on Mama too much. I wasn't good enough for Kevin, and now with Colin, it feels too similar.

I can't rewrite the narrative to make this anything more than what it is.

Just sex.

Blinking several times, I realize I've lost half an hour dwelling on something I can't change. When I glance down at my iPhone, there's a text from Colin.

Have fun with the Gems?

He cares? It's not like he and the Gems were friendly during high school, but I suppose he's making an effort, so I respond.

Great. Getting ready for the rehearsal dinner.

What time will it be over?

Meaning, what time can he come over for sex?

Not tonight. I need a clear head for tomorrow. I want to be present for Wynter on her big day.

I'm not sure.

He takes the hint.

Okay. Where and when should I arrive at wedding? You still want me to come, right?

My first thought is yes. But bringing Colin will restart the inquisition, will bring questions I'm not ready for.

Yet I already told the Gems he was coming, so there's no getting around it.

Yes. The wedding starts at 4. I'll see you after.

Sounds good. See you tomorrow.

I release an audible sigh. Tomorrow is going to be interesting. The Gems will not go easy on Colin or me. I've been there when we grilled Garrett and Blake, Egypt's and Asia's fiancés.

I'm bracing myself for a bumpy ride.

"You look beautiful, Wynter."

We're watching her reflection in the full-length mirror at the La Cantera Resort and Spa suite set aside for the bridal party.

Wynter is in a beaded off-the-shoulder lace ball gown with sequined appliqués adorning the bodice. Her usual waves have been pumped up with mousse, so they hang in soft curls to her shoulders. The makeup artist did a fabulous job with her. She looks glamorous yet tasteful, while her bouquet is simple with white peonies.

Wynter reaches for my hand. "Thank you, Shay. I'm so excited to join the Davis family."

"And we can't wait to have you. You've always felt like a sister to me, and now you'll be one in marriage." A tear trickles down my cheek at the love so evident in Wynter's eyes for my brother. My heart contracts. Although my marriage didn't work out and I put a big X over the words *love* and *relationships*, maybe there is hope love might find me after all?

"Don't start getting all sentimental and making the bride cry," Egypt admonishes. I don't take offense to Wynter choosing Egypt as her maid of honor; titles don't mean anything when it comes to the Gems. We love and support each other because that's what families do.

The door opens, and Mrs. Barrington walks in with her husband. She's in a floor-length navy evening gown, and her hair is done in a chic French-twist updo. Meanwhile Mr. Barrington looks dapper in a black tuxedo. His hair is closely cropped, but it's the look of pure love on his face that tugs at my heart. He's proud of Wynter. It's evident from the sheen in his dark eyes.

I'm jealous. I'll never see that look in my father's eyes. We don't have a relationship. I haven't seen him since I was fourteen years old. After the divorce, he tried sending for us after he moved away, but leaving Mama for any length of time, even for a weekend, was difficult.

Our father's new wife wasn't remotely interested in being a stepparent to two sullen teenagers. The visits stopped soon after they started, and the phone calls and texts dwindled until they were nonexistent. The only way I knew he was still alive was from the regular child-support payments. I guess we should have been happy he didn't totally abandon us. That money, along with the alimony, kept us from losing our house.

Excusing myself from the room, I go in search of my brother. He must be a nervous wreck. I find him in the groom's suite on the other side of the venue. I knock on the door and, after hearing his voice, enter the room.

Riley is in a white tuxedo with a black lapel and matching black trousers. He looks so handsome. He's pacing, about to wear out the carpet.

I walk over to him. "There's no reason to be anxious. You're marrying Wynter. The woman of your dreams."

"I know that here." Riley places his hand over his heart. "But tell that to my head." He points to his temple.

I laugh out loud. "Get out of your head. Tell me about your vows. Was it hard writing them?"

"It certainly wasn't easy," he responds. "It's hard to write how much I love Wynter, but eventually I found the words."

"There you have it. You and Wynter were meant to be." Leaning up, I cup his cheek. "Rejoice in that—you get to make her yours today and make her a part of our family."

Riley smiles down at me, and my heart fills with joy. One of us is getting our happily ever after. "How did I get so lucky to have a baby sister like you?"

I scrunch my nose. "Genetics?"

We laugh, and it alleviates some of the stress on Riley's face. Soon, his best man, John Russell, an intense man with a bald head and goatee who I've only met in passing, comes into the room. He, like Riley, is wearing a tuxedo, but his is black, the same as Mr. Barrington's.

"It's that time," John says.

"Let's do it," Riley responds.

Leaving them, I make my way back to the bridal quarters where the Gems are doing the most sacred of traditions. Something old. Something new. Something borrowed. Something blue.

"I guess that leaves me," I say, walking toward Wynter and grabbing both her hands. "Since you're joining the Davis family, it's only fitting you wear this baby's breath hair comb my grandmother wore when she married my grandfather and that my mother wore when she married my father." I tuck the comb into the side of her hair, ensuring it won't interfere with her veil.

Tears well in Wynter's eyes, and she tugs me forward. "Thank you, Shay. It means a lot to me. I'll wear it with pride."

Wynter releases me and smiles across at the other Gems. "Your presence here today is such a beautiful gift. I thank you for your love and support and your friendship."

"Enough schmaltzy stuff," Egypt replies with a smirk. "Let's get you over that broom."

Twenty minutes later, Wynter and Riley stand in front of more than three hundred guests and pledge their undying love. My eyes connect with Colin's. He's sitting in the middle row, his eyes focused on me. It makes me wonder what could have been—if he'd let go of his misconceived notions about the right type of woman, if I allowed myself to believe in love again. What a couple we could make!

Asia gives me a bump with her elbow and I return my focus to the ceremony, but I can feel Colin's eyes on my every move. I wasn't sure if he would chicken out at the last minute and make some excuse not to come. Men sometimes think women get ideas at weddings, but I don't. Although I want what Riley and Wynter have, that kind of love takes hard work. The feelings you have on the day you marry don't stay the same without perseverance. If Colin is expecting me to ask him for more than what he's offering, he'd be mistaken.

Yes, I like him.

Yes, I find him attractive and enjoy having sex with him.

But what the future holds is anybody's guess.

Twenty-Two

COLIN

I shift in the white padded folding chair. Not because I'm looking at the bride, though Wynter does look lovely. Instead, I'm entranced by one of the bridesmaids. Shay is stunning in a halter dress with an indecent side slit that has me thinking of the ways I'm going to own her later. All I have to do is shift it to the side, snatch off the thong I know she likes to wear and bury myself inside her.

The vows and promises Wynter Barrington and Riley Davis make are beautiful and poignant, but I try not to dwell on them and how they hit a bit too close to home in my current situationship. My thoughts, instead, are centered on how I'm going to fuck Shay when I get her alone. Maybe it's a good thing I'm distracted by sex, because coming to this wedding was not a good idea. All of Shay's friends are here. The rest of the Six Gems stand in a straight line beside

Wynter. They're all wearing the same color, but each dress is in a different style. I like that Wynter allowed everyone to be their authentic self.

There will come a reckoning with these women tonight. They're like a sorority of their own and fiercely loyal. Makes me wonder if I've given Shay enough credit.

A life with Shay would be high-octane. She keeps me on edge. She certainly isn't peaceful. She is turmoil and passion all rolled into one. Whenever I'm around her, I let myself lose control. If I'm honest, it feels good to let loose.

I keep hoping things will change, that she'll lose her allure. That if I gorge myself on her, the passion will lessen.

It hasn't.

It's only intensified.

And once this damn wedding is over, I'm going to act on it.

I watch Shay from the periphery. Taking photos with Wynter, the bridesmaids, the groom's contingent and then the entire wedding party, she never loses her smile or her zest for the occasion.

How does she do it?

By now, I'd be exhausted and ready to call it a day, but Shay has the same warm, sunny smile she's worn all afternoon. I want her alone so I can have my wicked way with her. Unfortunately, I have to wait until her wedding obligations are over.

Once the pictures are taken and the bride and groom have their first dance, Shay finally comes to find me at a table where I'm seated with several people from Riley's law firm.

I actually know one of them, having worked with him on a deal with the Myers Group. It doesn't go unnoticed she didn't seat me near anyone in her inner circle.

Was she worried about what people might say or think? I could care less. I invited myself to this shindig, and I'll sit where she wants me.

"I'm sorry." She bends down and whispers in my ear, "Who knew pictures could take that long?"

"It's fine. Don't worry about it. It's par for the course at a wedding."

"How about a drink?" She inclines her head toward the open bar in the corner behind the dance floor.

"Let's do it." Rising to my feet, I grasp her hand. We've only walked a handful of steps before several pair of eyes greet me.

The Gems minus the petite one.

And they are ready for battle.

"Shay, would you like to introduce us?" Teagan asks. Shay has shown me pictures of her friends so I'm familiar with each of them.

Shay tenses beside me, and I squeeze her hand reassuringly. "Gems, you all remember Colin Anderson. We went to high school together."

"Colin!" The surprise in Lyric's voice is evident, and I'm wondering what she knows that I don't. She stares at me with wide-eyed disbelief and then looks back at Shay.

"Colin, I don't know if you remember everyone, but this is Egypt, Teagan and Lyric. I don't see Asia, but she's around here somewhere."

"Probably in the bathroom," Lyric replies with a laugh. "She's had a tough time of it today."

"Anyway," Shay continues, "Colin and I recently reconnected at my studio. I'm helping him achieve some new life goals. Like getting fit and eating better."

"Is that right?" Egypt's eyes narrow, and I know she's not picking up what Shay is putting down.

"Yeah, I had a health crisis," I reply. "Shay graciously agreed to help me."

"So your relationship is professional? Platonic?" Teagan asks, and her eyes take in that I'm holding Shay's hand. I want to let go, like I burned something, but then that would be admitting we're doing something wrong, which we're not. We're two consenting adults.

"Teagan—" Shay starts, but I stop her. I'm comfortable telling them the truth about our relationship.

"Shay and I enjoy each other from time to time." I'm honest about what we are to each other, but then I hear Shay's sharp intake of breath. Clearly, I said the wrong thing.

"So you're fuck buddies?" Teagan goes in for the kill.

It would be unfair to answer that, but I guess my silence is more telling than not.

"If you hurt her—" Egypt moves forward until she's eye to eye with me, which in the heels she's wearing is pretty damn close since she's nearly six feet "—I will chop you up into little pieces and put you in the freezer of my restaurant."

"Damn!" Lyric smothers a laugh, and even Shay is taken aback.

That's when the petite Gem, Asia, comes up to our group

with her protruding belly. She walks around me several times and then says, "Do I know you?"

"You don't remember Colin?" Shay gives the same spiel about us going to high school together and that she's helping me get in tip-top shape.

"Ah yes, now I remember. You're in good hands with Shay. If anyone can fix you, it's her."

Asia winks at her best friend and then makes her way to the dance floor for the Cupid Shuffle. She motions the other Gems over. "Back off, ladies, and give them some room. What goes on behind closed doors is their business."

The darts the Gems shoot at me with their eyes should have killed me, but they take Asia's advice and rush off, leaving me and Shay blessedly alone.

"Did you have to say that?" Shay asks, folding her arms across her chest as she whirls around to face me. "'Shay and I enjoy each other from time to time'?" She mimics my deep voice, but it rings hollow. "It makes me sound pathetic and needy, and I'm neither of those things."

She spins on her heels and storms away.

I stare at her retreating figure for several beats. Honesty is the best policy, isn't it? But I suppose I could have handled that better. Why did I have to put my foot in my mouth and ruin a perfectly good situation? I used to be able to handle crises with ease, but lately I don't have a clue.

My medical scare forced me to check my lifestyle and take better care of myself, subsequently putting the kibosh on moving up the corporate ladder, on reconnecting with Claire, on everything I thought my father would have wanted for me.

Now I'm not sure where I'm headed. Shay is more than a casual fling. I care about her, and I didn't mean to hurt her.

How do I fix the mess I've made?

Twenty-Three

SHAY

Fury boils in my veins. Yes, my friends know Colin and I are hitting the sheets, but he said it so nonchalantly, so cavalierly.

There's a reason I haven't slept with many men. After Kevin, none of them moved me, not the way Colin does. I'm a slave to the emotions and endorphins rushing through me whenever we're together. I should have cut this off sooner, before we developed a bond, but it's too late. I'm in deep.

Yet to him, we're just frenemies with benefits.

Footsteps sound behind me, and I don't bother to see who it is. I *know* who it is because I sense him whenever he's nearby. When I walked down the aisle earlier, I didn't see him, but I *felt* him. When I finally stood by Wynter's side, I scanned the crowd looking for him. When my eyes landed on his, he was already watching me, assessing, lusting.

I spin around to face him. "Can't I have a moment alone?"

He steps back at my harsh tone. "You can, but I wanted to apologize for how I handled that—" he points back to the reception area "—discussion with your friends. I admit it wasn't my finest hour."

My eyes narrow. "You don't say?"

He walks toward me, but I don't let him touch me. Whenever he does, my mind blanks. If he touches me, I might let him off the hook. He needs to know where my boundaries are, because he just crossed one.

"I can't hold your hand?" He sounds offended.

"No, it's best if we keep our distance right now."

"Why, Shay? Are you afraid of your reaction to me?" he asks, coming closer.

I hold my hand up in protest. "I said stop."

He does. "Listen, I don't think I knew what to say when Teagan asked me. I thought honesty was the best approach, but now I realize you may not have wanted that level of honesty with the Gems."

"No, I didn't."

"I acknowledge I was wrong, okay?" Colin's voice is pleading. I want to forgive him, but I'm afraid to trust him. Every man I've loved has let me down: my father abandoned our family, Riley left me and Mama, and my own husband took off when the going got tough.

Then there's the Claire situation.

This is why I've focused on my work, on becoming a success: emotions are messy. I need to make room between us. Cool things off and give my heart some time to catch up with my head. Protect myself. I keep telling myself I just like Colin, but I suspect my feelings are deeper.

"Thank you." I nod. "I appreciate that. Why don't you go back to the reception? I'll be there shortly. I'm just going to powder my nose."

"Sure." He doesn't look as if he believes me, but I don't wait. I walk to the bridal quarters where I can have time alone to collect myself. Hopefully, when I come back I'll be less frazzled, ready to tackle the Gems' questions and opinions, of which there will be many.

When I arrive, the suite is a mess with clothes, shoes and robes everywhere. "Omigod!" I roll my eyes from the doorway. It's going to be a long night cleaning this up. I'm about to close the door when Colin steps into the room.

"What are you doing? I told you to go back to the reception."

"You did." He locks the door to the suite behind him and saunters up to me. "But I didn't like how the conversation ended."

"I forgave you." I clap my hands together. "It's over." I turn away from him, but he reaches for my hand, and within seconds I'm pressed against his chest.

Damn him.

I didn't want to be alone with him. Not now, when I'm wearing my heart on my sleeve. I haven't allowed anyone into my heart since my divorce. Yet somehow, Colin sneaked behind my defenses.

He's gotten to me.

He has the power to make me *feel* more than any man ever has. To make me want things from this transient relationship that I'll never get, like love, marriage, commitment, maybe even children. I try to push away from him, but he holds me tighter.

"I'm sorry, Shay," Colin says again.

"I heard you the first time." Defensive, I hold myself back. My nipples are turning hard as bullets, and I don't want him to know.

The skeptical expression on his handsome face tells me he knows I'm bullshitting. He keeps one arm wrapped around me and uses the other hand to grasp the back of my neck and pull me to face him. "I've been inside you, Shay. I know you're lying."

That makes me angry, and I push him away with enough force that it catches him off guard, and he stumbles backward. "Don't presume to think you know me because we're sleeping together, Colin. You have no idea who I am outside the bedroom."

"I thought that's what we agreed to."

"Yes, we did," I reply, "but you don't get to know what's going on in here." I point to my head. "My thoughts are my own."

"Except when you want this dick," he snaps back.

"Yeah, then and only then."

"All right," Colin says. "You want some of this dick now?"

"How dare you?" He has no right to say that to me. Not even if he's right.

He glares back at me. "You don't think I can't feel your nipples against my chest? That I can't smell your arousal? I may not know what's going on in your head, Shay, and yes, it's your choice to keep that from me. But I can read your body, and I know what it wants."

"You smug son of a bitch!"

"Tell me you don't want me, Shay. Right here and right now, and I'll leave."

We lock eyes, and I swallow the lump in my throat.

He knows I can't say it.

Damn him again.

Rushing toward him, I don't stop until my lips are locked to his in a hot and furious kiss. I push him against the wall. His hands grip my waist, and I clutch his shoulders while sliding my tongue into his mouth. If I was expecting a fight, I was wrong.

I'm met with heat.

The heat of Colin's tongue tangles with mine. My hands wildly tear at his clothes. I toss his jacket to the floor and scramble to undo his shirt buttons so I can touch his chest. Then it's on to his belt buckle and his zipper. I'm desperate to free him so I can show him who's boss.

Colin's hands are at the hem of my dress, and he's bunching the fabric at my hips so his hands can burrow beneath it. Then he's pulling the scrap of my thong aside and his long fingers are inside me, stretching me, getting me ready for him, but I won't allow him to run the show.

I push his hands aside and, within seconds, drop to my knees, wrap my hands around his length. Glancing up at him, I part my lips and take as much of him as I can down the back of my throat.

"Shit!" His hips push forward as I greedily suck him off. I use my mouth, my hands, my tongue and all the skills in my repertoire. Now that we've been together for nearly two months, I know what he likes, what he wants. I pull him from my mouth long enough to flick my tongue over the head of his dick, lapping up the beads of pre-cum from the tip. His head is thrown back against the door, and I release a throaty moan.

Then I lower my hand and take his balls into my mouth, gently sucking on them before returning to his dick. I swirl my tongue around it, applying the right amount of pressure and suction all while Colin grunts and pumps his hips faster and faster into my mouth. He's chasing his orgasm—the one that I, Shay Davis, who's never liked performing oral sex, is giving him.

He tenses, coming down my throat. I suck him dry and when I'm finished naughtily lick my lips.

"You minx." He reaches for his pants, which are hanging at his ankles and kicks them free. He grasps a condom from his wallet, tosses the wallet to the ground next to his jacket and dons the protection. Then he grasps me from underneath my arms, and before I can stop him he's lifted me and braced me against the wall. I have no choice but to wrap my legs around him and give myself up to my fate.

When he enters me, I gasp and my spine arches.

"Tell me you don't like this." He remains still, not moving inside me until I say something, but I refuse to speak. So he slams into me once again, and my muscles contract around him, trying to hold onto him.

One of his hands grasps my locs and tugs my head so I have to look into his eyes. "Answer me, Shay," he urges. "Tell me you want me."

"No, I don't." I don't know why I lie—I only know this punishment is one of the best I've ever received.

He drives into me again and then again. My eyelids flutter closed, and his body sets a rhythm, taking me closer to the end, closer to where I want to be.

But Colin is determined that I submit to him.

"Tell me!" he demands. My head lolls back against the wall, and my breathing hitches. As he thrusts deeper inside me yet again, I can't hold back. I say the words he's been waiting for. "Yes!" I scream. "Yes, I want you!"

Only then does Colin bury his head in my neck and groan out his release. We stay like that forever, our bodies pressed against the wall until our heartbeats slow and return to their normal rhythm.

Colin lowers me to the floor and my knees nearly buckle, but he holds me upright. "Are you okay?"

Nodding, I move away a fraction, using the wall as leverage. A glance in the mirrors shows I'm wrecked. My locs, once in an intricate updo, are now around my shoulders, and my makeup is smudged and my lips are swollen. I look like I've been fucked.

And I have been. Thoroughly.

Thankful the suite has a bathroom, I quickly excuse myself to freshen up. I thought I would show Colin I was in charge, but it's evident neither one of us is. We're both slaves to the explosive passion between us.

I've never found this kind of connection before. Why is this happening now? At nearly thirty years old with a relationship leading nowhere?

Eventually, after repairing the damage to my face and

sweeping my locs into a simple updo, I walk back into the living area of the suite. Colin is sitting down with his head between his hands. He looks up when I walk in the room.

"Hey." He stands when I move toward him. "Are you okay? I was kind of rough earlier."

"I'm fine. Good, actually."

A wicked smile crosses his lips. "*Good*? Shay, are you telling me you like it a little rough?"

"I guess I do."

"Duly noted." He takes my hand. "We should head back. Your friends probably think I've kidnapped you and will have police on the hunt."

I laugh. "They're not that bad."

"Ha! They were about to put me out to the firing squad for offending you earlier."

"As they should have."

Colin chuckles. "I suppose." He grasps my hand, and we walk back to the reception. The bride and groom are on the dance floor, and it looks like my brother is underneath Wynter's skirt.

I walk up to Egypt who is hugging Garrett on the periphery of the dance floor. "What's going on?" I inquire.

"Look who finally decided to join the party," Egypt replies. "We were looking for you. Wynter was ready to throw the bouquet, but she wouldn't without you. They're doing the garter first."

"I'm sorry. I was otherwise entertained," I whisper for her ears alone.

Egypt hazards a glance at Colin. "I don't need to guess

who with. I do believe you had a different hairstyle for the wedding."

I touch my makeshift updo. It's certainly not what the hair stylist created earlier. I blush.

Egypt pats my hands. "It's okay. Enjoy him, all right? It's been a long time since you've been with a man. Just be careful. Promise?"

"I promise."

And I mean it. I won't get carried away and find myself in love with Colin. I never want to be like Mama, destroyed if it doesn't work out between us. The feelings I've developed for Colin will lead nowhere. I have to accept that. I have my business and the love of my family and the Gems to support me. No matter what, I'll be okay.

"You caught the bouquet!" Wynter hugs me as if I've won the lottery. I'm stunned. I thought Asia or even Egypt would be the recipient, but me? My feelings are way too unsettled to think about marriage, especially with Colin.

"I think it's fate you caught the bouquet," Wynter whispers. "You could end up together."

I shake my head. "You're such a romantic, Wynter."

I don't burst her bubble, not on her wedding day, but I know better. Colin has never said he wants more than a friends-with-benefits situation, and that tryst in the bridal suite confirmed it. He only wants one thing—even if I'm starting to believe I want more.

Soon, the evening ends. Before Wynter and Riley leave, I take my brother aside. "Don't fuck this up."

Riley laughs. "I won't. Wynter is the best thing that

ever happened to me, and I never would have met her if it hadn't been for you. Thank you, Shay." Riley wraps me in the warmest of brotherly hugs.

When he releases me, I say, "I love you too, Riley, and I wish you both every happiness."

Seconds later, he and Wynter wave as they walk through sparklers and leave the reception. A moment of wistfulness comes over me as I watch their departure, until strong hands engulf my shoulders.

"They make a great couple," Colin whispers from behind me.

"Yes, they do." I turn to face him. "If you want to head out, you can. The Gems and I are ensuring the wedding planner gets all the help she needs to close out the evening."

He frowns. "Are you sure?"

I nod. "Go ahead. I'll see you on Monday." I can't be with him tonight. Our earlier encounter is still too fresh in my mind.

His brow furrows. "You're not coming over?"

"It's been a long day. Thank you for coming."

"Of course." His words are stilted. Is he angry? Then, to my utter surprise, he bends down and his mouth covers mine. Our tongues mate in a searing kiss before he lifts his head. "Good night, Shay. Ladies." He inclines his head, and I swivel to see the Gems staring open-mouthed as he walks away.

Lyric approaches me first. "I thought you guys were just, you know, friends with benefits? He doesn't kiss like someone who's in it just for sex."

"I'm going to have to concur with Lyric on this one," Teagan says. "Your Colin might just have a thing for you."

Even though she's five foot two, Asia pushes past them and over to me. "Don't believe the hype, Shay. If it walks like a duck and talks like a duck, it's a duck. If Colin says he only wants to be fuck buddies, then take him at his word."

"Damn, Asia. Do you have to be such a killjoy?" Lyric asks. "Maybe Shay wants to believe in happily ever after."

"Shay," I reply, "can speak for herself. And I know exactly where Colin and I stand. But I appreciate all of you being there for me."

"We got you, boo," Egypt says with a grin.

Later, after the Gems have changed clothes, ensured the extra food has been donated to a local shelter and checked that the bridal suite is clean, I head home weary and ready for bed.

After a shower and jammies, I recall everything that happened today. My brother marrying my best friend. Colin's introduction to the Gems. And finally, that heated encounter in the bridal suite that had Colin's dick in my mouth and my back against the wall with him deep inside me. My body still shudders at the memories.

As I am drifting off to sleep, I hear a ping from my phone. I glance down and see a text from Colin.

Had an amazing day with you today. Thank you for allowing me to share it with you, your family and friends.

His words slide their way into my heart.

It's a losing battle.

I've fallen in love with Colin.

Twenty-Four

COLIN

Ever since the wedding, Shay and I have retreated to our respective corners to figure out what the hell it is we're doing.

After our sessions, she doesn't suggest we go back to her place, and I don't offer mine.

The question that gets in my way: Why have I let *this* woman wrap me around her little finger?

The last couple of months, I've focused on my health and well-being and Shay, and I've made no moves to achieve my other goals. I've worked too hard to let up on the gas now, but that's exactly what I've done. Why?

Because I'm torn between wanting to make my father proud and following my heart.

Maybe the only way to figure out what's next is to talk to Claire. Figure out if she's truly the woman my dad thought she was. I've always thought Claire was beautiful and intelligent with a wry sense of humor. The chemistry between us was off the charts back then. Plus, she came from the right family, which appealed to me.

And so, here I am, meeting Claire for a drink. Initially, she was surprised to hear from me. It has been months since she first gave me her number. But after what happened at Riley's wedding and the connection with Shay I can't seem to shake, I need to give my derailed plans a chance to get back on track. I need to take control of whatever runaway thing is happening to my emotions.

So I'm at the country club waiting for Claire. However, before she arrives, I see Craig Abbott from the Myers Group.

"Craig." I stand up to greet him. "What are you doing here?"

"I'm meeting my wife for lunch. It's so good to see you, Colin. How've you been?"

"I'm doing well."

"You look amazing. Not so stressed," Craig says.

"Did I look that way before?"

"Maybe *stressed* is the wrong word, but you were intense."

"I was worried about the IPO. Matt told me everything went well."

"It did. There's been a few changes now that we're public, but you have nothing to fear. Your position is solid under the Family and Medical Leave Act."

I feel myself frown. "Would it not be, in other circumstances?"

Craig pats my shoulder. "No, no, that's not what I meant. Only that there's been a lot of shake-ups. You know that's to be expected when we're a publicly traded company. More people to answer to."

"Of course. If there's anything I can do during the transition—"

Craig waves me off. "Not necessary. We've got everything covered. You should take this time to get well and evaluate your life. Make sure you're going down the path that's right for you." And with those words, he shakes my hand and walks over to a woman with a chic blond bob who just walked in.

Despite Craig's attempt to reassure me, his comments have the opposite effect. Is my job in jeopardy? My promotion? I worked so hard at the Myers Group. I can't fathom all of it was for naught.

I need to figure this out, but then Claire approaches me. Statuesque at five foot nine, her honey-brown hair sways as she moves. Her oval-shaped face, arched eyebrows and cupid mouth are highlighted by the perfect makeup. She's wearing a belted shirt dress and high-heeled pumps. She looks nothing like Shay with her bohemian locs, makeup-free toffee skin and constant wardrobe of tank tops and leggings.

In the past, the sight of Claire all put-together excited me. But that was before Shay. Right now, I don't feel anything except fondness for an old friend.

I rise to my feet. "Claire."

Instead of accepting my open arms, she nods. I take the cue and pull out her chair. Once we're seated, I say, "You look beautiful."

"Do I?" she asks, peering at me.

"You know you do."

Claire always liked to be complimented on her appearance. When we were together, she spent a great deal of time and effort making sure she looked good whenever we went out.

She grins widely. "Thank you. Though, I must say I was surprised to receive the invite to lunch."

"Why?"

"I've seen you twice, first at your sister's and then at Vegan Avenue. When I didn't hear from you, I assumed you had moved on."

"Not at all," I say automatically, thinking *I was just consumed by a certain yoga instructor.*

"Are you sure? You were with Shay Davis. It looked like a date."

"It wasn't a date."

Her eyebrows rise skeptically. "If that's the truth, then I'm glad. I always regretted our breakup."

"You did?" My recollection of events is different. She was eager to date other men.

"Absolutely. You were always so intense and focused on the future. At the time, I wanted to live a little. We were much too young to be getting serious when we had so much life to experience."

I understand what she's saying, but back then it felt like way more than a first love. "And now?"

"I'm ready to settle down," Claire replies, "have a family of my own. I need someone like you, who has your life together."

If she only knew.

The last two months, my life has been anything but *together*—when I compare it to the plans Dad wanted for me.

Yet I've had more fun than I can ever remember having. And sitting here with Claire now, mulling over Craig Abbot's words, something feels off about all my plans and goals.

"I've done so much with my life since we were apart." Claire rattles on about everything she's accomplished over the last decade, from work to travel. During our entire lunch, she never once asks me a question about what I've been up to or how the last ten years have treated me. By the end of the meal, I'm exhausted by her chatter.

I find myself missing Shay, who knows how to be quiet in the moment. How to breathe and sit with silence. I've never had that peace with any other woman, including Claire.

"When would you like to get together again?" she asks as lunch ends and she wipes both sides of her mouth with the napkin.

"I have a busy schedule at work," I fib. I've found out what I needed to know. Getting involved with Claire would be a mistake. "Can I call you with some dates?" I ask out of politeness.

"Don't wait too long again, Colin." Claire stands. "If you do, you might find someone else has scooped me up."

I walk her to her car and tuck her inside. There's a moment when she pauses, perhaps for a kiss, but I push past it by looking away as I hold the car door open for her.

She pauses, seeming to recognize that things have shifted between us for good.

"Thank you for lunch," she says solemnly, as if she's saying good-bye. "I'll call you later." Though we both know she won't.

Then she drives away.

I stare at the retreating vehicle. Times have changed. I thought I could follow my dad's advice and everything would work out okay, but trying to live his dream has gotten in the way of my own happiness.

My feelings have changed.

My plans have changed.

I've changed.

And yet I still can't reconcile the maelstrom of emotions I feel toward Shay. What do they mean? Do I want more than just friends with benefits? Does she?

And if she does, what am I going to do about it?

Twenty-Five

SHAY

He's done it again.

Colin has pushed me away since the wedding just like he did after our run-in with Claire. Were the Gems and their expectations too much? Or was it the intensity of our sexual encounter?

Or maybe he's done with our fuck-buddies arrangement?

No matter the reason, the rejection hurts.

However, we agreed that when one or both of us were ready to call it quits, we would end it, plain and simple, while keeping our business relationship intact. I just assumed the sex would last as long as our ninety-day agreement.

And those feelings I've been harboring for Colin? They're more than just lust. They're love.

That's huge. I've been afraid, reluctant to love again... But I'm in love with Colin.

And I haven't even had a chance to talk with him about it.

That he doesn't feel the same is evident by how distant he's been since the wedding. Since the sexual encounter when I admitted to myself what I could no longer deny—I need him, *want* him, *love* him.

And now, I can't go back to how things used to be.

The next morning at the studio, I meet with an interior designer about the layout for the expansion. The landlord and I came to an agreement on the suite next door with money toward renovation, and I've signed a lease amendment. Now all I have to do is wait for the designer's plan, which she'll have ready in a few days, then I can send it out for bids to general contractors.

After the meeting, I'm heading to the locker room to change into my workout gear when Colin knocks on my door for our session. Since my meeting just ended, I'm still dressed in a blouse and slacks.

"I'm sorry I'm not ready yet," I reply, not looking at him. "Give me a few minutes to change." My emotions get the better of me, considering how he's been distant the last week. I try to push past him, but he grabs my arm.

"Shay, can you wait a second? I'd like to talk."

Don't look at him... If I do, I'll fall into the same pattern of getting caught up in the physical, like I always do.

Colin doesn't feel the same way about me as I do about him. I want to admit everything I'm feeling and beg him to love me, but I don't. I won't be like my mother, begging for my father's love.

I meet his dark chocolate gaze. "I'm on a tight schedule

today. Let me pass so I can get ready." Again, I try to leave, but he blocks my path.

"Surely we have a few minutes to talk?"

Inhaling sharply, I push on. "I'm sorry. I don't." This time, he steps aside allowing me to leave the office. Just because he's finally ready to talk about whatever is going on with him doesn't mean I have to drop everything. I have a business to run. The business that will still be around, even after Colin and I are over.

Five minutes later, when I emerge from the locker room, I'm still annoyed. My locs are in a ponytail, and this time I don't give a rat's ass what he thinks of what I'm wearing. I put on my most comfortable outfit—a medium-impact sports bra that reveals much of my back and high-waisted leggings that show off my ass. The leggings have a stocking effect that make me look snatched.

When I arrive at the private yoga room, Colin has already set out our mats, dimmed the lights and put on my favorite mood music. His attempt to win brownie points falls flat.

His disappearing act hurt. I'm going to make him suffer today, push him out of his comfort zone with harder poses.

I clap my hands. "Let's get started."

"I can't, Shay," Colin responds when I ask him to push up to bow pose several minutes later.

"Yes, you can. Just relax and give in to the movement. This will help increase your back mobility and strengthen your abdominal muscles."

"That's easy for you to say. You're not bent like a pretzel."

"Ha ha," I say without humor. "I'm doing the pose same as you."

He glances over at me and, in doing so, loses his concentration and collapses to the floor.

"Are you all right?"

"Is today some kind of torture routine?" Colin sits up and reaches for his towel to wipe the sweat off his face.

Something like that.

I've had him try some pretty challenging poses, such as praying mantis, *anantasana*, which has him lying on his side with one leg perpendicular, raised to the sky, the embryo pose, and *karnapidasana*, a plow pose with the knees covering the ears.

"I've gone way too easy on you. It's time we kick the level up a notch," I respond. "This next one is *bhujapidasana*. You're going to use your arms to balance yourself like this." I demonstrate the pose.

"You're crazy. No way can I do that," Colin balks.

Moving from my mat, I come toward him. "Yes, you can. Get into a low squat position with your feet slightly less than shoulder-width apart. Keep your knees wide."

When he's able to do that, I give him another step. "Now fold yourself until your torso is between your inner thighs. Place your hands inside your feet with your elbows touching the inside of your knees."

Colin manages this.

"Now snuggle your biceps underneath your thighs and place your hands flat on the ground on the outsides of your feet. Make sure the heels of your hands align with your feet." He's still trying and not complaining anymore so I push him further.

"Press your upper left arm and shoulder under the left thigh and leave your left hand flat on the floor. Now do the same on the right side." When he places his right hand flat on the floor, I know he's got this despite his protests to the contrary. "All right, now for the fun part. Engage your upper arms to maintain your balance."

I want to cry when I see him doing it. After all these months, he's able to do an advanced yoga pose.

"Squeeze your knees in toward your center. That's right," I encourage him. "Do you feel your upper back beginning to round?"

"Yeah."

"That's good. Place your weight on your hands, lean back, and lift your feet off the floor."

Colin does it! He's literally got his body weight up in the air while holding himself up by his bulging biceps, which at the moment are shaking. "Okay, I want you to stay here and breathe deeply for thirty seconds or for as long as you feel comfortable."

Lightly, I touch his shoulder. "Okay, release. One vertebra at a time."

When it's over, Colin falls back onto his mat. I bend down to look at him. "Great work—" But I don't get to finish my sentence because he's got me flat on my back on the mat.

"What the fuck was that, Shay?" His stormy eyes stare down at me. "Was that yoga or something else?"

I glare at him. "What else would it be?"

He jumps to his feet, about to leave, but he doesn't. He goes to the door and locks it.

Click.

"What do you think you're doing?" I push myself to a seated position.

"That's what you call foreplay," Colin replies. "Well, you have my attention, Shay."

He yanks off his tank top and marches over to me. His determination, his intention is unmistakable. I start scooting back, but I'm not fast enough. He reaches for my legs and pulls me to him. I'm weak when it comes to this man. Colin leans forward, his face so close to mine that I grab both sides of it and kiss him. He's surprised, but not for long. He takes ownership by kissing me hard and possessively.

His mouth leaves my lips, and I gasp for air, but that's just the start. He makes his way down my cheeks, my jaw and lower until he reaches my bra. He hauls it off without missing a beat, and then his hands wrench off my leggings. I want this, so much. All the worry and love I've been feeling since the wedding wells up inside me, desperate to be expressed.

The rasp of his beard tickles my inner thighs, then he's lifting my legs over his shoulders so his head is cradled between my thighs.

"Ah!" I moan when his hot, wet tongue laves my clit. He pleasures me until my cries ring out in the studio. Only then does he lift off me, but only so he can strip out of his clothes and don a condom on his straining dick.

This is crazy.

We're in my studio of all places, but I can't think straight.

He returns to me, kneeling. With his hands on my calves, he scissors my legs, pushing one right above my head while winding my other leg around his waist. I'm flexible, but I've never been in this position before. I'm open. It must be what he wants because he says, "I'm going deep, Shay, but you can handle it, right? Just like I handled those yoga poses."

Then he sinks into me, and I purr out the word. "Yes!" He edges in another fraction of an inch, pressing me into the floor and pinning me. "Oh God!" I cry out.

Deep isn't the word to describe how he fucks me.

He thrusts into me fiercely, and my body lifts off the floor, but he merely tilts back before surging into me again. The impact is so much I can't speak.

"You like that?" Colin demands.

"Yes."

"Can you handle more?"

"Yes."

He catches both my hands, placing them above my head, then he thrusts faster into me, grinding himself deeper and deeper, before pulling out and doing it all over again. He rides me until all I can think about is him. All I can feel is him. All I can see is him.

"Shay…damn, you feel so good."

His free hand grabs my leg, parting me farther, opening me completely. I shudder beneath him and eventually have no choice but to allow oblivion to come. I scream out in ecstasy. Dimly, I feel Colin start shaking, and then I hear his shout of fulfillment just as he drives deep and hard into me one final time.

Twenty-Six

COLIN

When she opens her eyes, Shay rushes naked from the private yoga room, uncaring if anyone might see her, and I hear the locker-room door slam.

Jesus fucking Christ! I scrub my five-o'clock shadow with my hand.

What the hell just happened?

Did I completely lose control?

Maybe so. One minute we're doing the hardest poses Shay's ever had me try. She seemed to be pushing me because I angered her by keeping my distance this week. Maybe those poses were her way of getting back at me, and maybe I deserved it. I've been so confused lately. But when she acted as if she weren't trying to push my buttons, I lost my shit.

I've never been this way with other women. I've always been in control of my body and mind, but not with Shay. I came at her with everything I had. The beast I didn't even know existed inside me was unleashed. Damn… I don't think I've ever been that aggressive with a woman before, but God, when I was deep inside Shay, it felt like I was home. *That* is terrifying. We were so connected.

I think back to when this whole thing seemed easy.

Claire would be my person, and Shay would be my fuck buddy. Yet somehow the script got flipped. Claire isn't the person I remembered. Or maybe she is, but I had blinders on. She is vain and self-indulgent while Shay is real, down-to-earth, genuine. I've seen it for myself. I've felt it. Shay truly cares about my well-being. Claire couldn't give a shit about me except what I can do for her.

Shay has found her way into my soul and lodged there. Despite my attempts to push her away or act like the connection between us doesn't exist…

What we have is red-hot. As evidenced by the fact I just dicked her down in the middle of her yoga studio. And I don't give a shit because when I'm with Shay I'm living in the moment. I'm fully present, not planning my next move.

All my life, I've been trying to be a success, to please my father. But he isn't here anymore. I have to start living for myself, start making decisions for my own happiness.

Once I'm dressed, I leave the private area. Thankfully, no one is here yet, so I walk to the locker room and knock on the door. "Shay? Are you all right?"

There's silence. I need her to answer me, so I know I didn't hurt her in my exuberance. She moaned and screamed my name. It felt like she was right there with me.

"Shay, please answer me. I didn't hurt you, did I?"

Her voice is faint, but I hear "No."

A sigh of relief escapes my lips. I'm glad for small mercies, but I don't want to leave like this. "Can you let me in? I'd like to see for myself that you're okay."

"No." Her response is loud this time.

"Okay, okay," I respond. "I'll leave, but I'll call you later." She doesn't answer, and I exit the studio upset with myself for acting like such a Neanderthal. Shay has lifted me up the last couple of months. Without her, I don't know where I'd be.

My thriving career, the one way I measured my success, was put on pause. Now I have to figure out my life, figure out what to do next. I've always had a plan, and now I'm floundering with no clear direction. Shay, and this intense connection we have, has me questioning all my life choices, questioning the direction I've been heading.

Needing reinforcements, I stop in and see Thea. A dose of reality and someone to talk to will be good. Then I'll call Shay.

I just pray she gives me the chance to make things right.

Twenty-Seven

SHAY

Once I think Colin is gone, I turn on the taps and get in the shower. My studio is my safe space, yet I let my anger overrule my better judgment in how I treated a client. How I treated the man I love.

But then, the lines with Colin have always been blurred.

Sleeping with him was my first bad decision. I wasn't looking for love or a commitment, so what was the harm? I thought I could focus on my business and enjoy sex with Colin, but no man has ever made me feel the way he does. Wanted. Desired. Needed. It's exhilarating. I got carried away.

Being with Colin is intense, powerful—it's made me realize I'm irrefutably head over heels for this man.

Even though he's point-blank told me I'm not the kind of woman he wants. Not the kind of woman who comes from the so-called right kind of family, with money and privilege.

To Colin, I'll never be good enough to rub shoulders with his elite crowd. He only wants me as his sidepiece.

For how long?

After showering, I put on the extra workout set I keep in my locker and stuff the other one inside. I can't look at it right now. When I open the door, I hope Colin isn't waiting for me. I count to three.

The corridor is empty.

I'm not teaching any classes. I lied earlier when I told Colin I was busy. Maribeth is instructing tonight. When I reach my office, I grab my purse and head to my car. I'm in the driver's seat when my phone rings. Mama is on the display.

"Hey, Mama, how are you?"

"Shay, I need you."

Her words send me into a tailspin. I've heard that tone of voice before. I know what it means. I know what's coming.

"What's wrong? What's happened?"

"It's Randy. He doesn't want to be with me anymore." She sobs. "He… he wants to explore other relationships. We've been together nearly two years. How can he do this to me?"

"It's okay, Mama." *Stay calm*. Reacting when she's upset will only escalate things. "I'll be over right away."

"I'm sorry, Shay." She's still crying. Could this lead her into a downward spiral? "How soon before you can be here?"

"Give me twenty minutes."

I hang up and immediately call her therapist. Dr. Murphy has been treating Mama for years and will know exactly how to calm her down. She tells me to bring Mama in for an appointment tomorrow morning because she has none this late in the day.

I pull into the driveway of Mama's house exactly forty minutes later, and my mother lets me know she's counted every minute. She greets me at the foyer in her robe. Her hair is uncombed, sticking up every which way. I can tell she's been running her hand through it. I remember this version of Eliza Davis. When my father left, she didn't leave the house for months. She stayed in her pajamas. She would sit by the window, waiting for him to return. My heart contracts in my chest. Not again. I *need* her to be well.

"You said you were going to be here twenty minutes ago," she says accusingly.

"I know, Mama. I tried, but traffic was a nightmare." I grasp her elbow and lead her to the family room.

We pass by the kitchen. There are dishes in the sink, pots and pans everywhere. *How long has she been like this?* I assumed the breakup was today, but her house tells a different story.

"You sure you weren't with that young man I saw you with at the wedding?" she asks when we sit on the sofa.

Colin is the last person I want to talk about right now. When I don't answer, she pushes me.

"Your date," she responds, looking at me. "You don't think I wouldn't notice? I saw the way he looked at you and vice versa."

"You're mistaken, Mama. Plus, we're not here to talk about me. Let's talk about you."

"I feel stupid." Mama's voice rises. "I believed everything Randy told me. I thought he loved me, but he doesn't."

Mama places her head in her hands, and I pull her to

me. "It's okay." I pat her back as sobs rack her body. This is the kind of devastation love can cause. This is why I don't want any part of it.

It has to be over between me and Colin. I would rather be alone, focusing on B&E, than experience this kind of heartbreak. I'm not willing to lay myself bare only to have him tell me again I'm not the one. He can have Claire while I keep my dignity. "It's going to be okay. He's not the only man out there."

"But he's *my man*," Mama wails, "or at least he was. He doesn't want me, Shay."

I understand. Colin doesn't want me either. At least, not for anything other than a roll in the hay.

"If he doesn't realize what a prize you are, Mama, then he's not the right man."

"That's easy for you to say, Shay. You're young. You have your whole life ahead of you. Do you know how long I was alone before Randy came into my life? Since your father left me? Nearly fifteen years. It's been awful." She starts crying again, and I grab the box of Kleenex I spotted earlier.

"Yes, it's awful, Mama, but you've been doing so good." I hand her the tissue box. "I'm so proud of you."

"How can you be? I've been a terrible mother, and I'm a terrible girlfriend." She pushes away from me and crawls into a corner on the couch.

This behavior, this black-and-white thinking, is why I called the doctor. Mama's mental health has been on the upswing for years. I'd hate to see her go through a bout of depression that could last for days, weeks or months.

"No, you're not."

“Then, why doesn’t Randy want to be with me?” she wails again. “I would do anything for him, Shay. I’ve bent myself inside out to be what he needs. Why? Because I didn’t want to be alone. How do you do it, Shay?”

“Do what?” My brows furrow in consternation.

“Be alone. Ever since you divorced Kevin, you haven’t had a serious relationship. Don’t you have needs? Don’t you want to be held, kissed…you know the rest,” she says with a half-smile through her tears.

“Of course I do, Mama.”

“That young man you were with is the first man I’ve seen you with in years.”

“I told you. I don’t want to talk about him,” I snap and jump up, heading to the kitchen. Opening the refrigerator, I grab a bottle of water and grab her medicine from the cabinet. “Besides, he’s not who matters. You do. I don’t like seeing you this way.”

“I’m a bad mother. I’ve never been there for you like I should have,” Mama says. “I was just so torn up when your father left. I thought my life was over.”

Returning to the sofa, I unscrew the cap and hand my mother the bottle of water and place a tablet in her hand. “Don’t say that. You’re much stronger than you think.” She takes the pill, washes it down and hands me back the bottle. I place it on the cocktail table in front of us. “Negative thoughts right now aren’t good. You’re a survivor. Remember that.”

“No, I’m not. I’m weak and pathetic.” She hangs her head low, and it breaks my heart.

Grasping both her shoulders, I lift her chin to face me.

"Don't talk like that. You're not pathetic. You have an illness, but you're managing it. You're strong, Mama." Dr. Murphy has told me in the past to give her positive reinforcement when she's going through a depressive episode.

"I don't feel strong." She leans sideways and rests her head on the couch. "I'm tired. Tired of wanting someone who doesn't love me back."

I recognize what Mama is feeling. I can't be with Colin if he doesn't love me. Attraction is not enough. Colin has made me crave something I haven't wanted in a long time.

A partner.

A husband.

Someone who won't care if I can't have kids of my own. Because *I* would be enough.

Colin isn't that person. He wants Claire, a woman he clearly idolizes as the perfect woman, and I refuse to feel less-than.

Like my mother, I'm a strong Black woman. Letting him go will be hard. But I don't want to be with someone who doesn't want to be with me.

I need someone who will choose me.

Twenty-Eight

COLIN

She's not home.

I've been waiting outside Shay's apartment for hours. I drove through the gate behind another car, and I've been sitting in my Audi.

Where the hell is she?

She's usually home after the studio closes, around seven at the latest.

Is something wrong?

Is she okay?

Of course she isn't okay, you asshole.

You fucked her on the studio floor, and she couldn't face you afterward.

She hid in the locker room and told me to leave. I didn't want to go. I wanted to talk to her. Explain that she's got me in such a state I don't know if I'm coming or going.

I've been with other women, but this is different. Like now. I'm worried if she's been in an accident. There's a feeling in the pit of my stomach that I know won't let up until I see she's safe. With other women, once I slept with them, I always went home to my own bed. Not with Shay. I like falling asleep next to her. I like waking up with her curled into my groin, my arm wrapped around her waist. I like that she gets up and makes us avocado toast, even though I don't like avocados. But she ignores me and fixes it anyway and makes sure I eat it. *It's a good fat*, she always says.

Being here makes me nervous. Scared. My plan was to have it all. Get fit. Go back to the high-powered, executive-level job. Marry a woman from the country-club set like my father wanted.

I'm throwing out that plan. I want a life *with Shay.*

I'm afraid of what it means—that I have feelings for a woman who was only supposed to be a friend with benefits. But I can't ignore that Shay *means* something to me.

I need to see where this goes.

When her car finally pulls into parking lot, I breathe a sigh of relief. Her car is several yards away from mine. She doesn't see me because she walks straight up the stairs to her apartment.

She probably wants her space, but I can't leave things the way they were at the studio. I have to check that she's okay. That I didn't hurt her, and I don't mean physically.

Climbing out of the Audi, I take the stairs two at a time.

Doubt makes me hesitate at her front door.

Will she slam it in my face? Will she send me away?

I don't know why, but something tells me she needs me. And I know I need her.

Inhaling deeply I knock, and I'm surprised when she opens the door without asking who it is.

"Shay, what are you—" I'm about to chastise her when I notice her red-rimmed eyes. "Shay?" I step in and pull her into my arms. "Baby, what is it?"

Grasping her face, I try to look at her, but she lowers her head to my chest and cries. That's when I close the door and walk us to her couch. Once there, I sit down, but instead of pulling her beside me, I pull her into my lap.

She doesn't resist. Thank God. I'm not sure why she comes to me willingly, but I'll take it.

I cradle her in my arms and let her cry. What's going on? What's upset her? I'm not so arrogant to believe it's about me. From her puffy eyes, it looks like she's been crying for some time.

I rub her back. "It's going to be okay," I murmur, just like she calmed me that night at the hospital. When she eventually quiets, she glances up as if she's seeing me for the first time. Panic ignites in her eyes, and I know it's because she was vulnerable with me. She jumps out of my lap and onto the sofa beside me.

"Easy." I shush her like she's a skittish foal.

She folds her legs crisscross. "I'm sorry for my meltdown."

A smile spreads across my lips. "It's okay. I have big shoulders." I flex my muscles. "I can take it."

She laughs a little, and it makes me feel better but not by much. I want to know what's got her so upset. "Want to talk about it?"

"Not really," she replies, "but Riley isn't here, so I guess you'll have to do."

I snort, not liking that I'm the fallback guy. I want to be her first call. "Um, okay."

She bends her head, and I can feel her thinking about what she's willing to share with me. I'll take whatever she's offering.

See? That's what I'm talking about. With another woman, I wouldn't care what's going on in her head, in her heart. With Shay, I want all of it.

"Go on," I say.

"My mother suffers from depression," she announces with no preamble. She watches for my reaction, and when I don't have one she continues. "I don't know how long she's been like this. Too long. But my earliest memories of it are after my father left her for another woman."

"What happened?"

"Mama fell apart. The sting of rejection was too much. She wouldn't get out of bed, shower, comb her hair or brush her teeth. It was bad, Colin."

"What did your father do? He didn't try to get her help?"

She rolls her eyes. "He didn't care. He'd moved on with another woman and was starting a new family. Riley and I took the lead in keeping our family together."

"And?"

"Riley was fifteen when the divorce happened. He became the man of the house and kept the bills paid, but then he got a scholarship to an Ivy League school back East."

"And he left you?" The question is out even though I know the answer.

She nods. "I was only fourteen when Riley left, and it was up to me to pay the bills, shop for groceries and generally keep it together while going to school."

"Shay, that's a lot." I never knew she was going through all this in high school.

Tears leak down her cheeks. "It was. I did my best, but sometimes..." Her voice cracks, and I don't hesitate to pull her back into my arms until she stops sniffling.

"Did you ever tell anyone, a teacher?"

"Why? So I could be put in foster care?" she says, lifting her head off my chest to peer at me. "Mama needed me. Plus, I didn't want anyone to know. I kept it to myself, except for the Gems."

"They were your lifeline?"

She nods.

"Now I understand why these women are so important to you. But I don't know how you managed it."

"Not very well. I was lonely, especially without Riley, so when Kevin, my ex-husband, started sniffing around when I was twenty, I fell for him."

"How long were you married?"

"Not long, a few years. Kevin couldn't take Mama's ups and downs because we lived with her. Plus, we were so young."

I sense there's more to the story that she's holding back. "But something happened today?"

"Yeah, Mama had a setback. She's been doing so well the last few years, Colin. Once Riley started making money as an attorney, he sent resources back home, and we were able to get Mama the help she needed. But today, the man she's been seeing broke up with her, and I swear..." I can see Shay trying to keep it together. "I saw her regressing, and I can't take it." She shakes her head, and tears fall from her cheeks. I swipe them away with my thumbs. "I can't go through it again, Colin. I can't."

"You won't have to. Riley is here. You won't be alone. Plus, you have me." She looks me at warily. "You do. I'm your friend, and if you need me, Shay, I'll be there."

She shocks me when she pushes me away and moves to the other side of the couch. I miss her next to me already. "We're not friends, Colin."

That hurts. "What do you mean?"

"We're fuck buddies, remember? But we're not friends." Saying it again is like she's digging a dagger deeper into my heart.

Now panic rises in *my* chest. "Stop saying that."

"Why?" she asks. "It's the truth. It's time we face it and stop burying our heads in the sand."

"About what?"

"That I'm not who you want, Colin," Shay says. "And I never will be. You want the Claire Watsons of the world. And that's fine. That's your choice, but I'm making mine. I refuse to be second-best, because I'm second to none."

"Shay..."

"I appreciate you being here for me tonight. You didn't have to come and check on me. You're a good man, but you're not *my* man. The man who loves me and wants me for me."

"You don't know what you're talking about."

"Can you honestly tell me otherwise? Are you going to say you want to date me for real? That you're interested in seeing where this thing between us could go?"

Yes. No. Maybe. I wanted to make it right, but now I'm back to being confused. I just know I don't like what she's saying so I strike back. "I've always been honest about what I wanted. What we were. What this was. It's not as cold as you're making it seem."

"It's exactly that cut-and-dried. We don't make love. We fuck. So let's end it right now because that's what we said we would do. When one or both of us decided to end it, it's over."

"What about my fitness program?" I'm grasping at straws. I don't want us to be over.

"It's best if we end that too," she responds. "You're well on your way to being fixed up. I've given you tools for your arsenal."

My chest constricts. I can't breathe. She's cutting off all ties with me. I don't want this, but I can't seem to get the words out.

"Since we still have a couple of weeks left, just consider us paid up, okay? You were overpaying me, anyway."

I shake my head. "No, I want to pay you. You need that money for the expansion."

She frowns. "I don't need your handout, Colin. The landlord is covering some of the construction and I have a little money saved up I can use if I need to."

"You shouldn't have to. We had a deal." I didn't come here tonight to end our relationship. I came to salvage it, to figure out the next step, but Shay doesn't seem to care. I don't understand. I thought she felt something for me. That night in the bridal suite told me we had a connection that was more than sex. Today in the studio, I felt it too.

This, right now—it has to be an act.

I don't know what to say to convince her I want her, but maybe my actions can do the talking for me. I slide across the couch and, with little effort, swing her into my arms and start walking toward her bedroom.

She yelps. "What do you think you're doing?"

"Let me show you we're not over yet."

She hesitates and then wraps her arm around my neck.

I can get through to her in the bedroom. My body will communicate just how much she means to me.

I don't want to lose her. I care about her. I'm going to change her mind and make her see she can't give up on us.

She can't give up on me.

Twenty-Nine

SHAY

One last time to remember him by.

That's what I tell myself when he lays me down on the bed and kisses me. Something tiny, tender and fragile bursts into life inside of me.

Colin shucks off his clothes and quickly removes mine. Then he's sliding into bed alongside me. Unlike earlier today, this time his touch is soft. He kisses the tip of my nose, then my chin, then he moves to my mouth and presses a long kiss against my lips.

His kisses grow more intense until eventually his tongue parts my lips hungrily. But just when I'm getting revved up, he slows us down, brushing his fingers along the underside of my breasts. Air hisses from between my teeth. All he has to do is touch me and my entire body comes alive.

When he dips his head to take my nipple in his mouth, I gasp out his name. "Colin."

"I know, sweetheart." He lifts his head and trails kisses to my ear where he tugs and teases me. Then he's moving to my other breast, lazily toying with it between his finger and thumb.

"Do you like that?" he asks. His tongue circles the sensitive bud before he suckles my flesh.

"You know I do." I don't tell him to stop because it feels too good. He releases my breasts from the heated embrace of his tongue to venture south, where I'm already wet.

My legs open wide so Colin can stroke me with his fingers, first one, then two, then I'm nearly undone. I need him. I must say the words out loud, because Colin brings his mouth to my sex to tease and lick me, whipping me into a frenzy. My brain empties, and I can think of nothing but the pleasure he's giving me.

It doesn't take long for Colin to bring me to the edge, but instead of taking me over he stops and levers himself upward so he can put on protection. Then he slowly sinks into me, all the way. It's heaven and hell because this is our last time together. I won't hold back. What do I have to lose?

He begins moving rhythmically, pressing forward, withdrawing, pressing and withdrawing. Ripples of pleasure build inside me, but I don't close my eyes, and neither does he. His eyes are dark as they peer into mine. I move with him, unrestrained in the fierceness of my passion and love for this man. Yes, *love.*

I was afraid to admit it to him in words, and not even with my body, but tonight I'm free.

Colin's thrusts become harder, faster, deeper. Each stroke builds my desire to a fever pitch. I can't tell where he ends and I begin. I don't want him to stop, so when he thrusts one final time I cry out as the entire world falls away, and my orgasm crashes over me in waves.

"I love you. I love you."

For tonight, right now, I'm free to express my feelings.

Colin's answer is a tortured groan of agony as he crushes me to him, pinning me with his hips. Then his whole body shudders with release.

Heat floods my veins, and I wrap my arms around him, pressing my lips to his. I'm closer to Colin than I've ever been with anyone. We've had sex often, but this is the first time it feels like we made love.

We're silent for several beats. I know he heard me. The words I haven't spoken in so long because I was afraid to feel them after my father and then my ex left me. Words I don't even think I meant during my first marriage but that I know without a shadow of a doubt that I mean now.

And it changes everything.

Colin pulls away from me to take care of the condom before returning to sit on the side of the bed. His back is to me, but I know what he's thinking.

I said the L-word.

The dreaded word that changes moments like these.

"How long have you felt this way?" Colin asks, not looking at me.

"I don't know." I pull the sheets up to cover my nakedness. My reply is honest but not what he wants to hear.

He turns to me, and his eyes dart back and forth as if he wants to escape. He'd rather be anywhere but here in this moment. There's regret in his dark brown eyes. My throat closes in my chest like I can't breathe because I don't want to hear the words that are coming next. Words that signal the end of our affair even though it's exactly what I said earlier that we should do.

"I'm sorry, Shay, but I don't feel the same way."

I nod. Even though I don't like his answer, I've said my truth. I don't have to lie to him or to myself. My heart aches, but I have always known I wasn't enough for Colin.

He rises to his feet and starts to dress. When he's done, he looks at me. "I care about you, Shay. You may not believe this right now. But you've changed me. Made me rethink everything. How I need to live my life for me and not my father. Who I want to be with. My entire future. We've never been just *fucking*. Even though you drive me crazy. I like you. A lot. You're amazing."

Damn him. Why does he have to be so nice when he's breaking my heart?

"I'm going to let myself out." He can because I gave him the code weeks ago because I trust him. Not just with my body, but with my heart, which is shattered.

I don't watch him leave. Instead I fall back against the bed. When I'm sure he's gone, I let out a heartbroken cry.

The sun rises the next morning like normal, even though my world flipped on its axis. I don't bother getting out of bed, which is something I've never done. I ask Dawn to cover my yoga classes and call in sick. I don't have it in me to be the positive Zen instructor my clients need.

I've become my mother.

And that propels me out of bed.

First, I rush naked to the living room to find my phone. Last night, I called a nurse and caregiver who agreed to stay overnight until Dr. Murphy could assess the situation. Wallowing in bed and thinking about my own failed love life is not an option, not when Mama needs me. She has an appointment with Dr. Murphy that's critical to ensuring she isn't taking a step backward in her recovery.

I check in with Nancy, Mama's caregiver, and all is well. Mama slept peacefully last night. That's a good thing. My shower is far from quick. As I soap my body, I recall Colin's mouth on my breasts, his hand between my thighs, his dick deep inside me as he made love to me.

He might disagree with the description, but we *did* make love last night. I know because I felt it. In the way he touched me. In the way he looked at me. In the way he reached into my very soul, the way we were joined as one. No matter how many times Kevin and I had sex trying to make a baby, I don't remember ever feeling that way with him.

Yet saying those three little words changed everything. Because, just as I suspected, he rejected me. Left me like every other man in my life has left me. I spoke my true feelings. I have nothing to hide. Now I'm cutting my losses and focusing on what I can control: B&E.

After the shower, I dress in jeans and a tank top and head over to Mama's. When I arrive, she and Nancy are seated in the kitchen, which is now tidy. But best of all, Mama looks like herself even though her eyes are a little puffy. Her long dark brown hair is in a ponytail, and she's wearing a peplum top with jeans.

"Hey, Mama." I approach her to give her a kiss.

"Hey, baby doll." She kisses my cheek. "Sorry about last night. I was so overwhelmed about the breakup with Randy. I didn't mean to worry you."

The golf-ball-size lump in my throat shrinks a bit. "I was worried, but I'm glad you're holding up. You look great."

"Nancy told me you made an appointment with Dr. Murphy."

"I did. I hope you don't mind?"

"Not at all. It's a good idea," Mama says. She's not fighting me, which is a good sign. In the past, she didn't want to see the doctor, but this morning I'm encouraged. Mama isn't as bad off as I thought.

Offering my hand, we head to the door and toward an uncertain future for both of us.

Thirty

COLIN

She loves me.

Shay loves me.

It wasn't an anomaly. I didn't misunderstand. She said the words *I love you* loud and clear. She wanted me to hear them, but I doubt she expected my reaction would be to tuck tail, run and hide?

But that's exactly what I did.

Love wasn't part of the plan. Love means losing control and not knowing what the other person will do. Love means the possibility of loss, like losing my father, and I've never gotten over losing the man I idolized. Yes, being with Shay has changed me, made me rethink my choices. But I don't like taking risks. I need to know what's coming next. For example, working hard at the Myers Group will take me to the next level. That's what I understand.

Love is scary. Love means letting go, even if you might fall.

I don't want to lose Shay, but I also can't say the words back. I care about her a great deal, but love? No. I shake my head. I don't do love.

In the past, what I thought was love was really just infatuation. Marrying the right girl and having a family was about my life plan. Love never factored into the equation.

And yet now that the word is out there, I can't seem to escape it.

Dammit if I didn't feel something last night.

When we looked into each other's eyes, when we moved together as one, I felt whole. And vulnerable. Scared. As soon as she said those three little words, I knew I couldn't stay. Even though I don't want to lose her, even though I went to her apartment to salvage us, I'm afraid to say those words to anyone.

Jesus, I have to get out of here.

Get back to work. That's where I'm in control. Where I won't have to think about all this messy love stuff. Instead, I can concentrate on numbers. There are no feelings or emotions when it comes to accounting. I'm nearing the end of my three-month medical leave, anyway. With my fitness regime ending, now is as good a time as any to find out where I stand at the Myers Group. Last I spoke to Craig, and even to Matt, a lot of changes were happening. It made me worried I might not have a job to come back to. And if I don't, what will I do then?

After a call to the HR department, I have an appointment later today to talk about my options. They don't know I intend that discussion to be in person. I won't stay in limbo about my career any longer. I put time and effort into moving up the corporate ladder, and I can't let it go without reviewing all options.

Pulling out my Brioni suit, I shine up my Ferragamo shoes and get ready to head into the office. I don't know what I'll face there, but I'm up for the challenge.

No matter what happens with me and Shay, she's given me this second chance to fix my life.

On the elevator ride up to the Myers Group, my heart palpitates and my hands shake. I tell myself it's just adrenaline. In the past, I was always excited to come to work. But the minute I set foot in the lobby, all the old stressors come back.

Breathe. Breathe.

Use the techniques Shay taught you.

By the time I get to reception, I've managed to calm myself. However, when I take a moment to notice my surroundings, I see the company looks completely different. The reception area has been given an impressive, modern makeover. Talking to Matt before I head to HR should give me a better idea of what I'm walking into.

"Good afternoon, I'm here to see Matt Harris," I tell the receptionist. She must be new, because I've never seen her before.

"And you are?"

"Colin Anderson."

She stares blankly at me. "I work here. I've been on leave for a few months."

"Of course. I'll contact Matt and see if he's available."

Taking a few steps past the reception desk, I peer across the open office. That, too, has been given an update with new carpeting and lighting. The large cubes are gone, and in their place are smaller workstations and collaboration areas with small sofas and tables. It looks more like someone's living room than an office.

"Mr. Anderson?" the receptionist says behind me. "He's on his way up."

Several seconds later, I hear Matt's voice. "Colin!" He looks genuinely surprised to see me. Is it really that shocking I'd want to come back to work? He knows me. I'm ambitious and want to keep moving upward. "What are you doing here? Isn't your medical leave not over for another couple of weeks?"

"Yeah," I respond, "but I figured I should come in, get the lay of the land and figure out where I fit in."

"Um, have you spoken with HR yet?" Matt wears a guilty expression.

I don't like it.

"No, I haven't. We have a meeting—" I glance down at my Rolex "—in a half hour. I was hoping you could walk me around."

"Sure, sure." Matt shifts from foot to foot. He's uneasy, and I'm not sure why. He walks ahead of me, and I follow behind him as he points out several changes. As we walk, I wave at several work colleagues, but most of them turn their heads and act as if they don't know me.

What's going on?

"You want some coffee or water?" Matt asks.

I grab his arm. "No, I don't want any coffee, Matt. I want to know what the heck is going on. Why is everyone acting so strange?"

Matt sighs. "We didn't expect you back for another couple of weeks."

"And?" I search his eyes for some understanding. That's when I notice where we are. "Where's my office?"

Matt lowers his head. "After the IPO, everyone was kind of reshuffled, and well, you don't have an office anymore."

"Excuse me?" My question comes out harsher than I intended. It's not Matt's fault. "Take me to Dan. I'd like to talk to him."

"Uh—um, I'm not sure if he's in today," Matt replies, and I can tell he's lying.

"Let's see." We start walking to the executive offices when I catch a sign on one of the doors. I stop in my tracks and stare at the nameplate.

Matt Harris. Director of Accounting.

My stomach drops. Did my friend steal my promotion? I turn to Matt, and his face is beet red. Now I know why he looked guilty. All this time, I thought he was my friend, but I guess the rivalry between us was never dead and buried. Instead, he's taken my dream job, the one that I earned, riding the coattails of my work straight to a promotion.

"I can explain," Matt starts, but I shake my head and take a step back. Tension rises inside me, and a migraine starts to form at the back of my head, but I remain silent as Matt's pleading voice becomes muffled in my ears.

All this time I've been working so hard on my health to come back to *this*? A company that couldn't even wait three months and allow me to get better before giving the promotion they all but guaranteed me to someone else? I understand Matt wanted to get ahead, but I'm angry he never told me, that he kept it a secret. I thought we were friends. And I'm livid that the Myers Group passed me over while I was out. I worked harder than anyone on the IPO for nearly a year.

My heart rate speeds up, my eye twitches, and sweat forms underneath my armpits. These are all the signs of stress I had before, when I worked here night and day trying to please the higher-ups, to please my father.

But I don't have to come back to this cesspool of a job that damn near gave me a heart attack. I can find another company. I'm highly qualified. If I want, I can strike out on my own and start my own accounting firm.

Either way, suddenly I know that I'm not coming back here. If they don't appreciate my hard work and ethics, then this isn't the place for me.

Turning on my heel, I head toward the exit.

Good riddance!

"Colin, wait!" Matt rushes after me. "Can't we talk about this?"

I spin around to face him. "What is there to talk about, you backstabbing piece of shit? That when I was on my sickbed, you went after the promotion I worked my ass off for? You mean talk about that?"

"Well, I…uh…"

I want to deck him, I really do, but he's not worth getting arrested. "Save it, Matt. I don't want to hear your justifications. I'm just glad I got a wake-up call before I gave my life to a company that doesn't give a shit about its employees."

My feet can't walk away fast enough. This is a blessing in disguise. There has to be something out there better suited to my talents, something that will allow me the work–life balance I seek, that I need. Maybe that's becoming an entrepreneur like Shay: she's certainly been an inspiration. What she's accomplished in the last year has been an amazing feat.

Tenacity and ambition, I've got loads of both, and I won't stop until I find the right fit. Because one thing I've never done is give up.

Thirty-One

SHAY

The next couple of weeks go by in a daze but not without drama.

When I'm not spending time with Mama, I'm at the studio, teaching classes or finalizing the Pilates expansion. I've secured a proposal for new equipment, and the general contractor has priced out construction for the addition. Work will begin soon.

I try not to think about Colin, try not to wonder what he's doing or how he's faring, but it's hard not to. I fell in love with him, with the way he believed in me and the expansion of Balance and Elevate. It was his ideas that helped make B&E's expansion profitable. I love his smile, his charm and how he knew how to please me in bed. Our last time together was everything I ever wanted. We made love. I know it in my heart of hearts. The way he looked at me, the way he touched me…

But our relationship is over.

Colin doesn't love me, and I accept that, but it still hurts. It feels as if I've lost something I'm never getting back.

The door to the studio chimes, and Wynter walks in looking radiant, happy and in love. She's in a strapless maxi dress with embellished sandals while I'm wearing my usual workout attire of a sports tank and yoga capris.

"Hey, girl." Walking over, I give her a big hug. "It's so good to see you."

"You too." Wynter squeezes my shoulders.

Since she and Riley got back from their honeymoon, we've tag-teamed spending time with Mama. Dr. Murphy said she doesn't appear to be regressing, but she may have some bad days. We've increased her sessions with the doctor to ensure she has someone to talk to about her fears and anxieties. It's working. Although she's sad about the breakup, she's not debilitated by it.

"Do you have time for a break?" Wynter asks. "I came up with our next girls' trip and thought we could grab a coffee."

Glancing down at my watch, I see it's eleven o'clock. Maribeth is teaching the class until we close at noon. "Absolutely. Let me grab my purse."

A few minutes later, we're pulling into a Starbucks to order. A chai tea latte for me and a caramel macchiato for Wynter. We find an empty table in the corner and head there with our drinks.

Once seated, Wynter stares me straight in the eye. "How are you really, Shay?"

"I'm fine." I sip on my chai latte. "How's Riley?"

"I'm not here to talk about Riley, though he's doing good. I want to know what's going on with you."

My brows furrow. "What do you mean?"

"The Gems and I are worried. The last couple of weeks we haven't seen you on the video calls. The only time I've seen you is at Eliza's."

"That's because I'm busy with the studio expansion. You know that."

Wynter nods and takes a sip of her beverage. "I do, but neither I nor the Gems think that's the real issue. There's more at the root of your unhappiness."

"I'm not unhappy."

Wynter gives me a look that tells me she knows I'm not being forthright. I sigh. "Okay, I'm a little sad, but I'll get over it."

Wynter reaches for my hand across the table and gives me a squeeze. "I felt this way when Riley said he didn't love me. I know the signs. That's why we need to have our annual girls' trip. It's long overdue. It would get your mind off Colin, and we want to do it now before Asia has the baby."

That brings a smile to my face. "I would love to see everyone."

Wynter grins. "Ah, a whisper of the Shay I'm used to. I'm glad to see she hasn't left."

I smile in response. "Where were you thinking for the trip?"

"We should keep it on the West Coast since Asia is due soon. A spa-and-wellness retreat at Canyon Ranch in Tucson would be good. You know, a spiritual and well-being rebirth, if you will. Egypt can't get away for a week from the restaurant so we're thinking of a long three-day weekend."

"Sounds fabulous." And exactly what I need. Maybe some meditation and long talks with the Gems will get me in the right headspace. "When do we leave?"

"How does this weekend sound?"

"So soon?" I reply, "I'll have to check with my instructors and see if they can cover my classes."

"If you can swing it," Wynter says, "it will be good for you. And while we're gone, Riley will hold down the fort with Mom. See? All the bases are covered. We just need you."

Tears well in my eyes. "Thank you, sis."

Wynter has no idea how much I need this. How much I need to get away, refocus and recenter myself and figure out how I move forward without Colin.

Several days later, I'm standing on the patio of a freestanding 2700-square-foot home at Canyon Ranch. They call it Casa Grande, and I can see why. As part of our stay, we received private transportation to the ranch, and a fruit basket, champagne, flowers and a variety of goodies were waiting for us when we arrived.

The home is spacious with a living room overlooking the Santa Catalina Mountains, a well-appointed kitchen, dining area, laundry, private patio, two master suites and a den that they've converted into a third bedroom. The girls and I will be bunking up for the weekend, but I don't care. This getaway is perfect.

"Shay, it's good to see you." Lyric comes up behind me

and joins me in staring at the beautiful vista. She's in the cutest khaki romper, and her hair is sideswept into a ponytail.

"How was the flight over?"

"Not bad."

"Good." My clipped response has her giving me a sideways glance.

"We've all missed you the last couple of weeks. You've been MIA for our FaceTime calls."

"I've had a lot on my plate." I knew if I joined the calls, they would know something was wrong, and I wasn't ready to talk, but I am now.

"Wynter told us about your mom. How's Mrs. Davis doing?"

"Better." I finally look at her. "I was worried she was having a setback. I don't think I could have handled it, not after—" I stop myself, but she catches on.

"Not after what?" Lyric asks, folding her arms across her chest. "Does this have anything to do with Colin?"

I knew I wouldn't escape their questions, but I hoped I could get through an hour, at least. No such luck. "Something like that."

"What happened between you two?"

"I want to know the answer to that question," Egypt says, stepping out on the terrace rocking a halter jumpsuit with a bottle of champagne in hand.

"Me too." Asia is right behind her with a bottled water. Since the last time I saw her, at the wedding, her belly has blossomed. But she's never looked lovelier. I'm happy for her.

"Shay isn't spilling the tea without us." Teagan and Wynter join us outside, each bringing glasses. They both are ready for the Arizona heat in a sundress and a tank top and shorts respectively.

And just like that, the Six Gems are back together again. Egypt pops open the champagne. Glasses are poured, and then we're holding them up. "To the Gems." We all clink glasses.

I'm midsip when the focus of the conversation returns to me.

"There is a question on the table." Asia takes a seat outside. There are only four, but I'm happy to stand so the mother-to-be can rest. "What happened with Colin?"

"We ended our working relationship."

Egypt laughs out loud, nearly spitting out her champagne. "Shay, c'mon," she says and glances around the group. "We all know you had more than an instructor–client relationship. Let's keep it real."

"Fine. We were sleeping together. The sex was hot, but I wanted more, and Colin isn't interested in being anything other than fuck buddies. So I ended it." I blurt out the words and then turn to face the mountains.

Lyric comes beside me and rests her hand on my shoulder. "Is it really that simple? Perhaps there's hope he will change his mind, and you can get back together?"

Lyric has always been a glass-half-full kind of person. "No." I shake my head. An errant tear escapes and runs down my cheek. "I'm in love with him, but he doesn't love me back."

"Oh, Shay!" Lyric circles an arm around my shoulder.

"To hell with him. You're the best thing that ever happened to him," Egypt states.

Several sets of arms come around me too until we're in a group hug. That's until I feel someone poking me.

"Would one of you guys stop hitting me?" I ask.

Asia laughs. "I'm sorry, Shay, but that's your overactive nephew in there."

My eyes widen as we pull apart. "He's kicking?"

"Yes, he is," Asia replies, smiling. She reaches for my hand and places it on her stomach. "He likes you."

"I hope so," I say, smiling through my tears as the baby inside her womb kicks again. Just as I'm accepting that Colin and I are done, I'm accepting that I may never have a pregnancy of my own. But I confess, "I can't wait to be Auntie Shay."

There's a ring of neither-can-I's. Talk of Asia's pregnancy and the baby take over, and we all move inside the house. I'm happy to have the heat off me.

"How are you feeling?" Wynter asks Asia.

"Like a big moose," Asia replies, rubbing her growing belly. "I can't wait for this little man to make his debut, because I'm not used to carrying all this weight. It's exhausting."

Asia usually weighs a hundred and ten on a good day. All you can see right now is the round belly on her tiny frame.

"You only have a couple of more months," Lyric says encouragingly, as if that should help, but the look on Asia's face says it doesn't.

"That's when the fun begins, Lyric." Teagan sips her champagne in one of the high-backed chairs. "Lots of late nights and early mornings." The living room has two large sofas and several chairs where we're all relaxing.

"Have you decided if you're going to breastfeed?" Wynter inquires.

Asia nods. "I'm going to give it a try. They say it's best for the baby. But there's something I need to share, and I'm glad we're here so I can do it in person."

"What is it?" I ask because Asia's face turns serious.

"Blake and I are married," she blurts out. She shows her left hand with an engagement *and wedding band*.

Egypt leans forward on the couch. "Say again?"

"Blake and I got married before your wedding Wynter," Asia answers. "After the scare with the baby, we declared our love, and we just knew we didn't want to wait for a ceremony so we had a private one with just the two of us, my mother and his aunt."

"Omigod!" Wynter's hands fly to her mouth. "I can't believe it. I'm so happy for you!" She rushes over and hugs Asia's shoulders.

"So am I!" Lyric does the same, and once again we're all in a group hug.

"I'm sorry I didn't tell you sooner, but Blake and I were carried away. We're so in love, and for a while there I didn't know if we'd have a future because I thought he only wanted the baby and not me."

"You don't have to explain," Egypt replies. "All we want is for you to be happy."

"That's right." I'm in agreement but also sad because now three of my friends are happy and in love. That leaves me, Lyric and Teagan in the singles squad.

"Wow! Okay, so I didn't see that coming," Teagan replies. "Does anyone else have any bombshells to drop this weekend?"

Egypt shrugs. "Not a bomb per se, but Garrett and I have decided on a destination wedding. Where everyone can come in for a few days, enjoy a beautiful locale, attend the wedding and go home."

"Sounds brilliant," Wynter replies. "Can I help you plan something?" As a travel blogger, Wynter travels extensively, and I'm sure she has lot of ideas.

"Of course," Egypt responds. "That's why I'm bringing it up. I need you to find Garrett and me our dream destination."

We continue chatting about updates in our lives. Teagan's brokerage business is doing wonders, and she's being named Phoenix's top real estate agent of the year at some awards dinner soon. The Gems promise to attend, except Asia because it's too close to her due date.

Lyric is surprisingly quiet while everyone is giving updates. I wonder what she's covering up. She always has a way of turning the focus and attention to someone else.

In the meantime, we walk over to Canyon Ranch's clubhouse where a private room is held for us. Wynter worked with them to provide us with a special menu. The dinner is divine as is the conversation with the Gems. Later, we return to Casa Grande and get in our pajamas to watch old movies like *Love Jones* and *Two Can Play That Game*. We stay up laughing and talking and reminiscing about days gone by until our eyes get droopy and we retire to bed.

Wynter and Egypt share a room. Asia and I are in another, while Lyric and Teagan are in the third. I'd hoped to share a room with Lyric to talk more with her, but Asia would wear Teagan out, so we're roomies.

"Tonight was so much fun," Asia said, once we've climbed into bed.

"It was. I needed this."

"You don't have to go through this breakup with Colin alone, you know. I may be with child," she says and motions to her belly, "but that won't ever stop me from being your friend and your sister."

I pat her hand. "Thank you."

As I drift off to sleep, I'm thankful to have the Gems. Being with them helps me see that I'll be all right without Colin. I can move on with my life. Falling for Colin showed me I'm capable of love—a deep, soul-stirring love that I feel all the way to the depths of my being.

Colin may have broken my heart, but he made me stronger too. Love, marriage and a family—all of these are possibilities.

I am still determined to make B&E a success, but I see now that it doesn't have to be work or love. I can have the things that matter most to me, if I'm true to my values, if I keep things in balance, if I consider what I need in each season of my life.

I just won't have any of those things with Colin.

Thirty-Two

COLIN

"I don't need to see you again for six months," Dr. Nelson says when he sees me at the three-month mark. After another round of lab work and an echocardiogram, the doctor is impressed. "Your turnaround is remarkable, Colin. I'm proud of you."

"Thanks, doc."

"I wish all my patients were as diligent about their health and wellness as you've been."

"If they were, they might not need you," I say, laughing, "but thank you. I worked hard to get here." After leaving his office, I head to my Audi and once inside lean my head against the headrest. I did it!

Ate right. Exercised. Did yoga and Pilates. Walked. And now I'm taking Pilates classes on my own. The workout has me using muscles I've never used before, a lot of core work.

And I went because of Shay.

Because I wanted to be close to her in some way.

Because I miss her.

That's hard for me to admit because I've never missed anyone I've dated, but I miss her smile and her positivity. She was a big part of my life for the last few months, and I can't shut off my feelings no matter how much I might want to.

Yet she wants nothing to do with me. Can I blame her?

She admitted she loved me, and I told her I didn't feel the same way. Couldn't feel the same way. Because I've never allowed myself to let go enough in a relationship to feel that emotion. But when I'm with Shay, control goes out the window. At least sexually. What would happen emotionally if I allowed myself to feel more than just lust and caring?

I've picked up the phone dozens of times to call or send a text.

To say what?

I need you.

Take me back.

I want to tell her about what happened with Dr. Nelson and the Myers Group. How I trusted Matt and he looked out for himself by taking a promotion that was meant for me. I want to tell her that I've thrown out the plan I had for my life, the dreams my father wanted for me. That I'm living for myself and doing what makes me happy.

With my skill set, I've been considering all my options. I contacted a headhunter, have some interviews lined up. I have enough money in savings to hold me for a while. Rather than resign, I allowed the Myers Group to offer me a severance package, which was substantial enough that I'm not worried about finances. They offered me the Assistant Director of Accounting job underneath Matt at my same pay with similar duties, absolving them under the Family Medical Leave Act, but I wasn't interested. I don't want to accept another position where I'm working myself so hard my health suffers. I need a job that will give me purpose but not take over. A job that will allow me time for family, friends and a love life. The thought of branching out on my own and becoming my own boss, like Shay, where my time and schedule are my own has its appeal.

And now that I'm headed into a life that feels more *mine*, I know who I want.

Shay.

I'm in love with her.

It took so long to figure this out! I let weeks go by. I let Shay think I couldn't love her. Why?

Because I was scared.

Scared of the feelings she brought out in me. Scared of being out of control. Scared of taking a risk. Of losing someone I love.

But I don't want to be afraid anymore. I want to embrace life.

I want a life with Shay.

Will she take me back after the way I've treated her? If I were her, I would slam the door in my face. But that would be me. Or at least the old me.

But that's not Shay.

She's given her mother grace, even though it was hard growing up and she had to give up so much. She's forgiven

Riley for leaving her to care for their mother alone. She's moved past her divorce to embrace being with me, *loving* me.

Shay is capable of forgiveness.

I'm just hoping she's willing to forgive *me*.

Thirty-Three

SHAY

Our girls' trip was exactly the reset I needed. Canyon Ranch was the transformative setting I hadn't known I was looking for. The sadness stayed behind in Tucson, and what's ahead are the possibilities.

I'm prioritizing my needs.

And that begins with getting the Pilates addition to the studio built. Once that's done, I'm going to start dating again.

Am I ready now?

Absolutely not. I'm still in love with Colin, but after some mindfulness sessions at the ranch, I've accepted that I can't change him. I can't make him love me even though I may wish he did. But I *am* deserving of love. Worthy of love. And I'm going after it.

After the incredible two and a half months we spent together, I rediscovered my sensual side. A side I never fully explored during my marriage while we were trying for a family. Now I know what I like and what I don't. And for that, I have Colin to thank. I'll be ready for the next man, who will love me as I deserve to be loved.

And so, after saying goodbye to the Gems at the ranch, with promises to be there for Asia's son's birth, Egypt's destination wedding and Teagan's awards dinner, Wynter and I make our way home to San Antonio.

The next morning, I'm at the studio ready to take on the day. My classes are back-to-back because Maribeth has the day off after taking over for me this weekend at the last minute.

I prepare for my beginners' class like I always do. I lower the lights, flip on the lavender diffuser and turn my phone to some calming music. My clients slowly filter in. I'm shaking out my mat and setting up my bolster, pillow and other props when I notice Colin standing in the back of the room.

My heart stops.

I can't breathe.

What is he doing here? He's not dressed for a workout. He's in jeans and a T-shirt. I don't think I've ever seen him dressed so casually.

He looks good, but then he always does.

It's only been a few weeks, but he looks even better than I remember. And damn, my body reacts, remembering him.

Remember what you learned in Tucson. Center yourself. I walk toward him. "Colin, why are you here?"

"I need to see you."

"I'm about to start class."

"I don't care. This can't wait. It's urgent."

Concern washes over me. "Is everything okay?" I grab his arm. "Is it your heart?"

He nods.

Omigod! Quickly I move toward my office and turn to the crowd forming. "Give me a few minutes, okay?"

Once in my office, I quickly close the door and start checking his pulse. It's racing. "What's going on? Do you need to lie down? Are you feeling faint? Should I call an ambulance?"

"I miss you, Shay."

I cock my head to peer up at him. "What did you say?"

"I miss you."

"Colin, for Christ's sake, I thought there was something wrong with you." I step toward the door, but he places his palm against it, blocking my exit.

"My timing sucks," Colin says. "I know that, but I have to tell you about my journey here, my journey to you." My look of ambivalence seems to unnerve him because he pauses before continuing. "The angina taught me that I have to take care of myself and not let work consume me. I have to find the right balance of ambition and staying the course with my health. You didn't just teach me yoga poses, Shay. You taught me to put myself first. A job will always be there, but my quality of life is what's important. I was given a second chance to make things right, to spend time with my family. With my father gone, my mother and Thea look to me as head of the family. And working so hard, I missed out on being there for them."

"I'm glad you've come to these realizations, glad I helped you destress and put yourself and your family first," I respond, "but if that's all..."

He shakes his head. "That's not all, Shay. I have to say this before I lose my nerve because I've never said it to anyone else."

"Oh yeah, and what's that, Colin?"

"I love you, Shay."

His words knock me back, and I stumble into my desk. With his quick reflexes, he catches me before I fall, and just like the first time we touched, electricity shoots through me.

"You feel it too, don't you?" Colin says, looking at where our hands are still joined. "It hasn't gone away, and it's not going to."

"I—I have a class," I stammer. "You…you can't come in here after all these weeks and say these things to me. Not when I'm trying to get over you."

"I don't want you to get over me, Shay," Colin says.

"Of course you do," I spit out. "Because I'm not the woman you want. You want to be with Claire, or someone like her. I've never been more than a passing sex partner to you."

I can see that my words gut him. Colin shakes his head furiously. "That's not true. Yes, the sex between us was amazing—*is* amazing," he clarifies. "My desire for you has always overwhelmed me with its intensity. I got scared."

"Don't you think it scared me too? You've always made it clear we were a temporary thing. You wanted your ideal woman. And like I told you before, I won't be second-best, not even for you."

"And you're not. You're my first, second and third choice," Colin replies. "I made the worst decision of my life letting you go. My father had a plan for my success.

He drilled it into me. But that plan failed, and none of it means a damn thing without you, Shay. You make me lose control in the best way. You're my future. Please tell me it's not too late."

Colin is saying all the words I've longed to hear. Tears brim at my lids. I glance toward the door where my students are waiting for me to start class and then look back to the man I still love.

And without a second thought, I leap into his arms.

Colin catches me, folding me into him. Oh, it's bliss, such bliss to be in his arms again. And when he bends down to kiss me softly, tenderly, sweetly, I melt.

When he finally lifts his head, I say, "I love you too, Colin. I never stopped."

"Oh, thank God!" He leans his forehead against mine. "Because I want your love, Shay. All of it, for the rest of my days." The voices outside my door get louder. "But you should get out there. Your students are waiting, and heaven forbid I stop someone from getting their fix-up."

I smile at him through my tears. "Allow me to tell you that your ninety-day fix-up is officially over, Mr. Anderson. You've been upgraded to the title of Boyfriend."

"I happily accept," Colin responds with a wide smile across his incredible mouth. "I don't want to waste another minute without you in my life, Shay."

Brushing my lips across his, I rush out to my class. My students are waiting, several of them with knowing looks, as if I've been up to something naughty in my office. If Colin and I had had more time, that might have been the case, but not today.

Maybe later.
We have time.
Because Colin confessed his love, and so did I.
This isn't my happily ever after, it's just the beginning.

★ ★ ★ ★ ★

Look for Lyric's story,
Going Toe to Toe
Coming August 2024!